A ROYAL AGENTS OF MI6
CHRISTMAS NOVELLA

FIND MY ANGEL

BOOK FIVE

USA TODAY BESTSELLING AUTHOR

HEATHER SLADE

FIND MY ANGEL
© 2023 Heather Slade

979-8-88649-376-4

MORE FROM AUTHOR HEATHER SLADE

BUTLER RANCH
Kade's Worth
Brodie's Promise
Maddox's Truce
Naughton's Secret
Mercer's Vow
Kade's Return
Butler Ranch Christmas

WICKED WINEMAKERS
FIRST LABEL
Brix's Bid
Ridge's Release
Press' Passion
Zin's Sins
Tryst's Temptation

WICKED WINEMAKERS
SECOND LABEL
Beau's Beloved
Coming Soon:
Cru's Crush
Bones' Bliss
Snapper's Seduction
Kick's Kiss

ROARING FORK RANCH
Coming Soon:
Roaring Fork Wrangler
Roaring Fork Roughstock
Roaring Fork Rockstar
Roaring Fork Rooker
Roaring Fork Bridger

THE ROYAL AGENTS
OF MI6
Make Me Shiver
Drive Me Wilder
Feel My Pinch
Chase My Shadow
Find My Angel

K19 SECURITY
SOLUTIONS TEAM ONE
Razor's Edge
Gunner's Redemption
Mistletoe's Magic
Mantis' Desire
Dutch's Salvation

K19 SECURITY
SOLUTIONS TEAM TWO
Striker's Choice
Monk's Fire
Halo's Oath
Tackle's Honor
Onyx's Awakening

K19 SHADOW OPERATIONS
TEAM ONE
Code Name: Ranger
Code Name: Diesel
Code Name: Wasp
Code Name: Cowboy
Code Name: Mayhem

K19 ALLIED INTELLIGENCE
TEAM ONE
Code Name: Ares
Code Name: Cayman
Code Name: Poseidon
Code Name: Zeppelin
Code Name: Magnet

K19 ALLIED INTELLIGENCE
TEAM TWO
Coming Soon:
Code Name: Puck
Code Name: Michelangelo
Code Name: Typhon
Code Name: Hornet
Code Name: Reaper

PROTECTORS
UNDERCOVER
Undercover Agent
Undercover Emissary
Coming Soon:
Undercover Savior
Undercover Infidel
Undercover Assassin

THE INVINCIBLES
TEAM ONE
Decked
Edged
Grinded
Riled
Smoked

THE INVINCIBLES
TEAM TWO
Bucked
Irished
Sainted
Hammered
Ripped

THE UNSTOPPABLES
TEAM ONE
Furied
Merried

COWBOYS OF
CRESTED BUTTE
A Cowboy Falls
A Cowboy's Dance
A Cowboy's Kiss
A Cowboy Stays
A Cowboy Wins

Table of Contents

1

Z

Before walking out of my flat, I checked my reflection in the mirror for the countless time. Tie was straight, suit looked okay, hair seemed grayer than the last time I checked, but at my age, that was to be expected. Some of it had to do with the job I'd just left.

Chief of MI6. It had been my sole professional aspiration for as long as I could remember. And, truth be told, I'd loved every minute of it. Until recently.

While some might think it was the birth of my second grandchild or watching the team of agents I oversaw fall in love, marry, and start families of their own that made me realize my job was no longer enough, it wasn't any of that.

When I looked up and saw the woman I'd invited to dinner tonight pass by my office, it was as though something inside me snapped.

Leighton "George" Marietta had captivated me from the moment I first met her. She had deep pools of cognac-brown eyes and long, wavy dark brown hair that cascaded over her shoulders. How I wanted to weave my fingers in its soft waves.

Each time I passed her in the hallway, I struggled to keep my eyes from drifting to her lush breasts, her gloriously long legs, and her arse I longed to cup with both my hands.

In the four years since we met, neither of us had truly acted on our mutual attraction. Talked about it, yes. Succumbed to it, no.

Sure, there had been flirtations here and there, but it never went further. More than once, we'd agreed a relationship between us was inappropriate, given I was her boss, then eventually, her boss' boss. A couple of times, I'd initiated the conversation. Once or twice, she did. However, no amount of denial, resolve, or statement of impropriety had changed how much I wanted her.

At one point, I convinced myself "out of sight, out of mind" was the best course of action. However, it had only resulted in absence making my heart grow fonder.

And while, in this day and age, others felt no shame in crossing those lines, I couldn't. If it meant I'd lose the chance to know her better when she found another man who wasn't bound by duty in the way I was, I'd have to live with it. Or so I used to think.

That all changed today when I picked up my phone, called the man I reported to, and resigned from my position with SIS—His Majesty's Secret Intelligence Service.

As soon as that call ended, I walked out of my office, down the hall to hers, and knocked.

"Come in," she said, her eyes widening when she looked up at me.

"I've resigned," I blurted.

George raised her brow and studied me. "Have you?"

I nodded. "Effective immediately."

She sat back in her chair and folded her arms. "Now what?"

"I was wondering if you'd like to celebrate over dinner tonight. With me."

George smiled. "I suppose it wouldn't be much of a celebration if you weren't there. Is there a group gathering—"

"No. Err, forgive my interruption, but this celebration has nothing to do with work." I cleared my throat. "I'm asking you on a date, George."

It dawned on me that she might turn me down. Perhaps she'd run out of patience with me years ago.

I let out the breath I'd been holding when I heard her say, "I accept."

Now, five hours later, I was on my way to pick her up. I had quite an evening planned for us. First, dinner at her favorite Indian restaurant, which just so happened to be my favorite as well. Afterwards, I intended to invite her back to my townhouse for an after-dinner cocktail. Or, if she preferred, her place. Either way, now that I'd decided to pursue her, I wanted George to know it would be full throttle, as they say. I wanted her in my life and in my bed. Starting tonight.

I looked out the window and saw the car service I'd hired pull up. After grabbing my overcoat, I took one last look in the mirror. "Do not talk yourself out of this," I said to my reflection.

After locking up behind me, I walked down the steps to the car, checking the time on my mobile.

"*Puck?* What are you doing here?" I asked when I saw him waiting in the backseat.

"Hello, Z," he responded once I was inside with the door closed.

I looked down and saw he had a gun pointed at me. "What in the bloody hell is the meaning of this?"

"I need your help with something."

"For God's sake, Puck. All you had to do was ask. This…this…"—I motioned to the gun—"is not necessary. I insist you explain yourself immediately, followed by exiting the vehicle. I have a previous and urgent engagement."

"'Fraid that won't be possible, sir."

"Agent Lindstrom, I demand you lower your weapon—" Before I finished my sentence, the car sped off.

"Now, hand over your weapons and your mobile. I'd rather not, but if you force me, I will kill you, Z."

I stared down the barrel of his gun, knowing I had no choice but to do as he said or prepare to die.

2

George

There was simply no way I could've gotten the time wrong. I was a bloody MI5 agent, for God's sake. More, I'd spent the last four years waiting, wishing, hoping for this day, or night, rather, to come.

Z and I had danced around each other, so to speak, since the first time we met. When our flirtations felt like they were about to turn into something more, one of us would pull back, remind the other a relationship between us was inappropriate, and for a while, we'd avoid each other. That would last a few days, sometimes longer, until we couldn't stand it anymore and struck up yet another *innocent*, usually work-related, conversation.

I paced between my flat's door and the front window, watching for Z's arrival. As of right now, he was ten minutes late. Z was never late. It was one of many reasons I was attracted to him. Punctuality. Professionalism. Respectfulness. Charm. The thick mop of silver-gray hair I was forever tempted to run my fingers through. Perfectly tailored clothes that hugged his broad shoulders—and exemplary backside. And bright blue eyes that had sparkled when he finally asked me on a date. The date that was supposed to be taking place right now.

I checked my mobile. Another five minutes had passed, and I hadn't received a message from him, explaining his delay.

There was no way I'd accept he'd merely changed his mind. After all, the date was one impetus for his decision to resign as chief of MI6—Military Intelligence, Section 6.

I'd never seen the man as giddy as he was earlier when he'd sauntered into my office, leaned forward, and rested his hands on my desk, then told me he'd resigned.

I'd raised a brow.

When he added that it was effective immediately, I'd asked what was next for him, fighting against my temptation to jump up, throw my arms around him, and kiss him the way I'd wanted to almost from the moment we met.

"I was wondering if you'd like to celebrate over dinner tonight. With me."

"Is there a group gathering—"

When he clarified it was a date, I immediately accepted.

I'd agreed without a moment's hesitation, and yet, here I was, waiting on the man again.

At the twenty-minute-and-counting mark, I sent a text. At twenty-five on the dot, I rang him. At thirty, I called my boss.

"George? What can I do for you?" asked Pinch Fulton, Director General of MI5. "Aren't you supposed to be—"

"Sorry to interrupt, but Z hasn't shown up." Not wanting to jeopardize either my job or our potential relationship, I'd informed Z of my intention to apprise the DG of our plans. Z, who was as forthright as anyone I'd ever known, agreed it was a prudent idea.

"He hasn't shown up?" His stunned tone reinforced my own disbelief. "I fear something has happened." I heard jostling in the background. "I've accessed tracking"—something he had the authority to do and I did not—"his last known location is in the opposite direction of your flat."

"The restaurant where we have reservations is between his place and mine."

"Hmm."

"What?"

"GPS shows his mobile is in an alleyway. No doubt smashed to bits, given it stopped transmitting approximately thirty minutes ago. I'm headed to the Cross and have issued an all-call alert."

My mobile vibrated. "Got it. Headed there now."

"Copy that."

I was already on my way out by the time Pinch rang off.

When I arrived at Vauxhall Cross, headquarters for the UK's Secret Intelligence Service, Pinch was already there. I cringed when Wren Whittaker, Z's daughter, walked in a few seconds after I did.

The woman was absolutely entitled to be there, to know her father might be in danger. However, she and her husband, Wilder, who'd been MI5's interim DG before Pinch and who I'd also worked for, had a six-month-old baby girl.

Wilder had given me my code name. My last name was Marietta, and he'd initially called me Georgia. Eventually, it was shortened to George.

Wren approached and put her arm through mine. "How're you holdin' up, George?" she asked. Unlike her father, who had been raised in the UK, Wren grew up in Texas, where her mother was from, and she had a definitive Texan drawl. While I wouldn't consider Wren a close friend, we were more than acquaintances.

"I'd ask you the same," I said.

"Worried, but not more so than you. I gotta tell you, I've never seen my daddy as excited as he was when he called me earlier today."

"I'd no idea he was so unhappy at MI6," I murmured, looking over at Pinch, who was studying his phone.

"MI6 has nothin' to do with it, George. He was excited about your plans tonight."

"It was just dinner," I said almost in a whisper.

Wren shook her head. "That's not the way he saw it. To him, it was the beginning of a new life. I shouldn't tell you this, but…"

"But *what*?"

"Z asked me to pick up some things for him and deliver them to the townhouse."

"Things?"

"Clothes. For you. So if you, you know, ended up back at his place, you wouldn't feel uncomfortable, you know…after."

I was mortified. "Wren, I'm so sorry. I'd no idea—"

"Please don't apologize. The point I'm trying to make is that I've never heard my father sound as happy or excited as he was about your date. When I say that, for him, it was the beginning of a new life, I mean it. He wanted a life with you, George."

My heart clenched, and I blinked away threatening tears. I'd shared his eager anticipation and was fraught with worry for him. My heartache was profound, thinking that something horrible may have happened to him when we were right on the verge of finally being able to explore the attraction between us. "Excuse me," I muttered, hurrying to the loo, knowing I could no longer stop my tears from falling.

"Where in the bloody hell are you, Z?" I said out loud once I was certain there was no one else in the restroom.

3

Z

Once the vehicle we were in entered a less-populated part of the city, the masked driver pulled to the side of the road. Puck kept his gun aimed at me while the other man exited the car, came around to the back passenger door, blindfolded me, then bound my wrists and ankles. He removed my mobile, watch, wallet, and firearm—all four of which Puck was aware of—thus eliminating all but one tracking option someone could use to locate me.

Puck held up his SIS-issued mobile. "Under his right arm," he muttered.

The man who'd bound me opened two buttons on my dress shirt, reached through the short sleeve of my undershirt, and felt beneath my arm, removing the small disc affixed to my skin.

I couldn't see his face, and there was nothing else I recognized about him. My best guess was he worked for another intelligence agency. Until he spoke, if he did, I'd have no way of determining which it might be.

It occurred to me Puck's mobile had been discovered on the Maltese island of Gozo. Apparently, he'd transferred his tracking information to another unit, which was the one he'd left behind. Also obvious was that any other tracking devices he'd had were either disengaged or destroyed. And that meant his disappearance and my abduction were premeditated.

Based on the direction we'd traveled from my flat, ascertained before I was blindfolded, and the length of the remainder of the drive, I suspected I was being taken somewhere in the vicinity of Northampton.

The city was the southernmost tip of what was known as the golden triangle of distribution, given ninety percent of Britain's population could be reached within a four-hour drive. The significance of which was that the area contained close to one hundred and fifty thousand square feet of warehouse space—making it an ideal place to hold someone captive.

Upon our arrival, I relied on other senses—smell and hearing—to gather mental clues as to where we were. The white noise intrinsic to constantly running machinery, along with the slight ammonia or sulfur smell associated with diesel exhaust, substantiated my theory regarding our location.

Before dragging me from the vehicle, the driver removed the rope binding my ankles. He and Puck led me through a creaky, heavy metal door and into a musty-smelling building, which was mostly empty, based on the way our footfalls echoed.

Once inside, I was escorted several paces to another door that didn't sound as though it was made of metal. When I heard it close behind us, Puck removed the blindfold before the second man pushed me onto a cot. A single chair was the only other thing in the room. The lock clicked when both men exited.

I lay on my back, wrists still bound, and stared up at the ceiling, wondering when Puck would divulge whatever it was he needed my help with so desperately that he'd kidnapped me—the man who, until earlier today, was the bloody chief of MI6.

Regardless of whether I'd tendered my resignation, my disappearance would be investigated at the same level as a high-ranking diplomat. Perhaps even as a royal. Given Puck knew this, it made me more concerned about his mental state.

It would be nearly impossible to track the passage of time without windows to see out of; however, there was a chance that there would be an increase in noise in the immediate area, signifying work hours.

The doorknob jostled, and I swung my body around and sat up. When Puck entered the room, I glared in his direction. "Either end this now, Lindstrom, or be prepared for things to go very badly for you."

There was a gray pallor to his skin, and his hair was longer than I'd ever seen it. He was also in dreadful need of a shave. His eyes met mine, and in them, I saw anguish and fatigue.

"I cannot, sir," he muttered.

His use of the honorific made me think he was truly looking for guidance from me. "You said you needed my help."

He looked over at the wall and appeared to be fighting a display of emotion.

"Someone very important to me is missing."

The irony nearly had me shaking my head in irritation. People I was important to were likely in a state of panic presently—namely George, although by now, I was sure she'd alerted her boss at MI5, at the minimum.

Puck had been missing too, and there were people, myself included, who were very worried about him.

"How can I help?" I asked rather than point any of that out to him.

"I haven't figured that out yet."

I sighed. "Sven, I need to reiterate that this is not the way to go about getting assistance. Let's return to Vauxhall Cross, where you'll have the full backing of both MI5 and MI6."

"There's an inherent problem with doing that."

It was everything I could do to tamp down my anger. "Go on."

"You believe she's dead."

"Puck, are you talking about Seshat?" I didn't just *believe* she was dead. She'd been shot and killed just yesterday when our team raided a warehouse much like this one, where Oleander had been taken hostage by Seshat herself.

His eyes filled with tears he attempted to blink away. "I met her at university. Oxford, in fact. She's bloody brilliant."

I lowered my head and rested it against my chest, feeling the pain of his loss radiating off him as I heard him leave the room again.

I'd met my wife at the very same university. There were times when it felt like it had happened yesterday, and others, when it seemed a lifetime ago—which it was.

We were practically children when we first met. Looking back, it was hard to fathom that ten years later, she was gone.

***

I walked into the lecture hall, disgruntled that I had to attend a class on my birthday, particularly since it was mind-numbingly boring. Three hours spent listening to a professor drone on about quantitative reasoning usually resulted in many of the thousand students in the theater dozing off.

Given I'd arrived only a couple of minutes before the class started, there were few seats to be had, and those were near the front of the rotunda.

"Pardon me," I whispered as I made my way to an open seat that was, of course, near the middle of the row. When the woman seated next to it looked up at me, my heart nearly stopped. She was the most beautiful person I'd ever seen. Her wavy blonde hair fell past her shoulders, and her eyes were a haunting gray-green. She took my breath away.

"You should probably take a seat," she whispered when the professor stepped up to the podium and I was still standing, likely with my mouth hanging open.

"You're American," I said, exhibiting my less-than-brilliant reasoning abilities. "Apologies," I mumbled, taking my notebook out of my satchel.

When she didn't respond, I glanced over at her. The smile she bestowed on me was the best birthday gift I'd received in my life.

"I'm Katherine," she whispered.

When I responded with, "Archer," the person seated in front of us shushed me. I looked at Katherine again and was gifted with a second heart-stopping smile.

I fell in love that day. I might not have realized it at the time, but recollecting the very moment it had happened made it indisputable.

From that day on, mid-September through November, Katherine and I spent as much time together as our individual schedules would allow. I learned she was from Texas, where her family owned a very large ranch. I was also schooled in the etiquette of asking its size. Which, apparently, one should never do. Still, she graciously informed me it was over one hundred thousand acres—something I couldn't begin to comprehend.

When Christmas rolled around and it was time for her to return to Texas to spend it with her family, I fell into a funk. I managed to hide it from her, or at least I believed I had, but my mum was another story.

"What's got you so glum?" she asked when I arrived for our weekly family dinner. She cupped my cheek. "Let me guess, it's a girl?"

I rested my hand on hers. "A woman, but you're right."

She pulled me over to the table and patted one of the chairs. "Tell me what's the matter."

"Mum, like she is a woman rather than a girl, I am a man. This conversation is inappropriate."

"Pishposh. You're never too old to talk to your mum about anything."

"She's from the States."

My mother raised a brow.

"Which means she's leaving on holiday."

"Ah. I see."

"Forty-two days."

"Yes, I recall."

My mum and my father had both graduated from Oxford University. In fact, it was where they'd met as well.

"She didn't invite you along, is that it?"

I shook my head. "That would be equally inappropriate. We haven't been seeing each other that long."

"You could always take your own holiday. See the sights."

I rested against the chair. "I cannot. She'd think…" What? That I was crazy? Perhaps that I was a stalker?

"She'll think you care so much about her that you won't be able to wait over a month to see her."

"I'll appear desperate," I muttered under my breath.

"Desperately romantic, I'd say."

"What's this?" my father asked, patting my shoulder before joining us at the table. To my chagrin, my mother reiterated our entire conversation.

"What say you, my darling?" she asked him once she'd finished.

One thing I loved about my parents was their unabashed love for each other. You could see it in their eyes whenever they were in the same room.

"You didn't tell him I did the same thing with you?" he asked.

She smiled, and her cheeks turned pink when he reached over and held her hand. "I was about to, but I think you should."

"You can always blame it on Christmas," he said.

"What does that mean?" I asked.

"You know—the spirit of the season, and all that. Admit you got carried away by the joy of the holiday."

One look at him, and I knew that was exactly what he'd done.

"Of course, America is a bit farther than the Cotswolds."

When my mum's parents were still alive, we spent every holiday there too.

"A bit, but it isn't as though Archer has to travel by steamer. It's a few hours' plane ride." She turned to me and rested her hand on mine. "You know that's when your father proposed?"

"Mum!" I gasped. "I hardly know the woman. Please don't suggest such a thing!"

"It would certainly make for a lovely Christmas memory."

I left England for Texas on the twenty-third of December without any intention of proposing. Yet it was precisely what I did.

4

George

The electronic evidence boards, typically dark at this time of night, lit up as agents from both MI6 and MI5—all of SIS, really—walked into one of the situation rooms at Vauxhall Cross. It was the largest by far, usually used for cases of great magnitude. Things like terrorist bombings, threats on the lives of the prime minister or members of the royal family, and now, the disappearance of the former chief of MI6.

The majority of those in the room not only outranked me, but their years of experience far exceeded my own.

"Most everyone I sent the all-call to has arrived, with the exception of Nemesis and Ares," said Pinch, addressing all those assembled. "I've briefed Benjamin Coffey, the UK Foreign and Commonwealth Development Secretary, as well as Prime Minister Pelham. If either receives a ransom request, I will be notified immediately." He looked over at Wren. As Z's daughter, a ransom request might come to her as well.

"I called Quint on my way here. He said he'd be on the lookout. He also said he'd brief Decker."

Quint Alexander was Wren's older brother, and Z had adopted his best friend, Decker Ashford, when they were both teenagers. While Quint hadn't followed in his father's footsteps in pursuing a career in intelligence, Decker, like Wren, had.

"They're on their way, as is Darrow," she added.

Darrow was Quint's wife and also Wren's husband, Wilder's, younger sister.

"How are you holding up?" Wilder asked.

"Managing," I said, barely above a whisper.

The kindness Wilder and Wren had shown me was remarkable. They were the ones who should be tended to. From what everyone else knew, Z and I had no more than a professional relationship. Outwardly, we'd behaved as friends, but privately, I longed for something more. Something I'd hoped would change tonight. Z had been clear about it being his intention as well.

I squared my shoulders, refusing to allow myself to sink into self-pity. I was here, at SIS headquarters, safe. Z was *somewhere* else and undoubtedly in danger.

I checked the time. A little past twenty thirty hours. Ninety minutes after I waited near my front window for Z to arrive. Each tick of the clock mattered in cases of disappearance. Every second made a difference.

I approached Pinch when I heard him call my name. He motioned for me to take a seat beside him. When I did, he pointed to the electronic board immediately in front of us.

On it were pins indicating Z's residence, mine, the restaurant where he'd made dinner reservations, and the last known location of his mobile. When Pinch zoomed in, I could see the pin I'd thought was just the phone was actually multiple objects.

"Whoever has him knew what to look for," he muttered. "They know the inner workings of SIS."

Double agents were rare in this day and age. Intelligence technology had advanced to the point their existence was *nearly* impossible. However, there was a glaring absence in the room tonight, and Pinch knew it as well as I did.

He turned to me. "Puck."

I nodded. He'd been missing almost a full year, and even though the entirety of SIS had looked for him the same way they were now looking for Z, he'd seemingly vanished.

The most logical supposition was he'd been recruited to work with AMPS, the organization being investigated by the United Nations Coalition Against Human Trafficking. Seshat, the woman Puck had allegedly been romantically linked to, was killed in a raid last night when an agent working on the case was rescued after being abducted.

Tracking Seshat was how they'd found the woman—Oleander. That in itself was troubling. Why hadn't Seshat done a better job preventing us from tracking her in the same way Puck had?

"We've received footage from the overheads," said Wilder, nodding to a board on our left. Z appeared on the screen, exiting his building and getting into a nondescript town car. Zooming in, it became apparent the identifiers on the vehicle had been intentionally hidden and the driver was masked. "We should receive more from where Z's mobile and other devices pinged in South Tottenham momentarily."

Within seconds, those videos appeared on the same screen. The driver, still wearing the mask and gloves, exited the vehicle, walked around to the opposite side, and opened the rear passenger door, the view of which was obscured. "This is all we've received thus far," Wilder reported. "Reconnaissance is working to find more. In the meantime, I suggest we send a team to that location immediately."

"They know what they're doing," Pinch muttered for the second time as he typed something into his mobile. Seconds later, four of my colleagues collected their gear, checked their firearms, and left the situation room.

Wilder nodded. "Whoever has Z covered their tracks down to the letter, as they say."

I followed his gaze over to his wife, who was studying her mobile. "Wren?" prompted Wilder.

"Somethin' is nigglin' me," she said, glancing at him briefly. While the woman wasn't as active in intelligence as she had been prior to getting married, at one time she'd been considered the preeminent agent in the world. So much so, her very existence was often questioned. Many said "Wren" was a compilation of at least three operatives, perhaps more.

"What, my love?"

"Seshat made too many mistakes."

When I'd initially read the report detailing what went down last night, I thought the same thing. At first, I wondered if the agent had been blackmailed into abducting Oleander, thus leaving clues for a quick discovery. However, she had to have known she faced death by doing so, and she had, in fact, been shot and killed during the raid.

"We're missin' somethin'," Wren added. She'd looked away from her mobile, but her gaze didn't appear focused. Watching as she processed information was fascinating, regardless of the fact I had no idea what she was thinking.

Pinch zoomed out, and a series of rings appeared on the electronic board. The outermost represented how far someone being transported by car could've traveled based on the time when the overheads captured both Z initially getting in the vehicle as well as that of the driver stopping in South Tottenham. From there, the most likely route would've been to travel via M1 northwest to Luton, where there was an international airport. Beyond it, Northhampton marked the southernmost city of the largest warehouse district in all the UK.

"This is a bit of good news," said Wilder. "The NRO has not picked them up at London Luton."

Which meant Z was not on a plane headed God knew where.

"I need everything we can find on Seshat," said Wren, looking first at Wilder, then at me.

"Roger that," he said, glancing in my direction.

"Go ahead," said Pinch when I looked at him before following Wren's directive.

I stood and picked up my laptop, then walked over to the table where Wilder and Wren were seated.

"What are we looking for? Anything specific?"

"I'll know it when I see it. And, Wild?"

"Yes?"

"When I say 'everything,' I mean go all the way back to when and where she was born."

5

Z

"About Seshat…" I began when Puck returned.

When he shook his head almost violently, I ceased talking.

He paced the room. "You let Mithras slip through your fingers." His eyes bored into mine. "The entire op was executed by people who had no business crafting it, resulting in the loss of two of my agents—Beak and Vulcan."

Puck had personally recruited Jamie "Beak" Thomas and Tracy "Vulcan" North, who were both killed in the line of duty during a shootout on the island of Gozo. It was where we'd tracked a known human trafficker who operated under the name of Mithras. Puck was right to say he'd slipped through our fingers that night. However, I did not agree it was due to a poorly crafted plan.

"I planned to propose."

I'd dropped my gaze, but my head snapped up at the abrupt change of subject.

"At the conclusion of the op. I'd requested leave."

This was news to me, not that Puck reported directly to me. Axel "Pinch" Fulton was his boss at MI5, and as a member of the UK task force, he reported to Cayman.

"What were your plans?" I asked, knowing the more I could get Puck to talk to me, the better I could determine his mental state.

He looked down at the ground, then up at me. "I was going to do it on Christmas." He stood and walked toward the door, rapping once. It opened, and right before he walked out, he turned back around. "I'd hoped we'd marry on New Year's Eve." The door closed, and I heard it lock from the opposite side.

Puck's words hit me hard. It was exactly as Katherine and I had done. Was he aware? Was he intentionally toying with me by drawing correlations between my relationship with my late wife and his with Seshat?

I shifted my body, lay on my back, and looked up at the ceiling. After a while, I closed my eyes, recalling one of the happiest times of my life.

***

The entirety of the flight from London to Dallas, then from there to the closest airport to the King family's ranch, I worried I'd made a dreadful mistake. Once

I landed in Austin, I rang Katherine. If my fear proved correct, I'd catch the next return flight.

"Merry Christmas Eve, Archer!" she answered, making no attempt to hide her delight in hearing from me.

"Katherine." Her name was like a prayer on my lips. "I've a surprise for you."

"You do?"

I took a deep breath, but before I could say anything else, Katherine spoke. "Last night, I made a Christmas wish."

"Will you tell me what you wished for?"

"Tell me your surprise first."

"According to the gentleman at the car rental agency, I'm approximately one hour from your family's—"

"Are you serious?" She squealed. "You're here?"

"Good surprise or no?"

"The best—it's what I wished for."

I let out the breath I hadn't realized I was holding. "Did you, really?"

"I swear it, Archer."

"Shall I wait until the day after tomorrow to pay a visit?"

She laughed. "And spend Christmas alone? Don't be silly."

"I don't want to intrude on your plans."

"Archer, I *literally* prayed for this."

While Katherine was thrilled by my surprise visit, her father, or Daddy as she called him, wasn't.

Two things worked in my favor, though. First, Katherine was an only child, and just in the short amount of time I'd spent with her parents, it was clear their daughter's happiness was paramount. Second, her mother appeared to like me from the moment we met.

"Q will come around," Mrs. King said when the man left the house, using tending to his ranch business as an excuse.

"Q?" I asked.

She smiled. "It's short for Quad, my husband's nickname."

"My daddy is the fourth Samuel Kennedy King," Katherine explained. "His father was the third, and his granddad was junior." She leaned closer to me. "His real nickname is Wasp; it's only my mama who calls him Q."

"What about you, Archer?" Mrs. King asked. "Are you named after your father?"

"I'm not. His name is Thomas," I said, chuckling. "My mother's father was William. However, her maiden name is Archer."

"Ah, so *Archer* Alexander."

"That's correct."

"Hmm," Katherine's mother murmured, making me wonder where she was going with this conversation.

"My mama is hellbent on giving everyone a pet name," Katherine whispered.

"Yeah? What's yours?" I asked when her mother appeared distracted, writing something on a notepad.

Her cheeks flushed. "Boring."

I smiled. "I find that hard to believe."

Her cheeks turned even more pink. "K."

"Z!" her mother exclaimed. "Look." On the note-pad, she'd written Archer, then Alexander, then Zander. "It's that or A."

"I like it. Z, I mean." Katherine looked up at me. "Yeah?"

When she smiled and nodded, I knew that regardless of what her mother came up with—even something as disparaging as donkey—if it put that look on Katherine's face, I'd forever refer to myself that way.

"Can you ride?" Mrs. King asked.

"She means horses," Katherine whispered.

I smiled. "I have a time or two."

Their facial expressions were identical—both had furrowed brows.

"Sorry, teasing. I've ridden since I was a child."

"How well?" Mrs. King asked.

I shrugged. "Fair, I'd say."

"Now is *not* the time to be humble, Z."

"I am a member of the Ashbury Park Polo Club, as was my father before me."

"Have you competed in the Park Open?"

I was stunned that Mrs. King was familiar enough to ask. "I have."

"Last year?"

"Yes, ma'am." It had been the first time a British team won the title in several years. We'd emerged victorious in the final round after defeating the Americans.

She put her hand on Katherine's arm. "Best not to tell your father."

"Understood."

"Shall we, then?" Mrs. King asked, looking at me.

"Yes?" I had no idea what she meant, but I surmised I should agree, no matter what it was.

"Good. Again, no mention of the Open. In fact, perhaps it would be best to avoid the topic of polo entirely."

"Are we riding?" I asked Katherine when her mother walked out of the house.

When she turned to me and smiled, every thought other than how I wanted to tell her I loved her left my head. I did get the impression that proving I was a decent horseman would go a long way in gaining Katherine's father's approval in advance of confessing my feelings.

"Our guest will ride Unbridled," Mrs. King announced to the waiting groom. The man raised a brow but turned to fetch the animal. "My husband probably suggested Willie saddle up Rosebud."

Katherine smirked. "Or Apollo."

"Bore him to tears or kill him."

I raised a brow at Mrs. King's statement. *Kill* me? Truthfully, there weren't many horses I could recall that frightened me. I'd not challenge fate, however.

"I'm sure your family is missing you this holiday," Katherine's mother commented when we'd been riding for several minutes.

"It was their suggestion I visit, actually."

When she raised a brow, I looked over at Katherine, whose smile once again unnerved me.

"Why is that?" Mrs. King asked.

"My father did something similar one Christmas."

Both women smiled.

"I like your father already," Mrs. King murmured. "Here we go," she added a moment later. I followed her gaze and saw Mr. King headed in our direction.

"We were hoping you'd join us, Daddy," Katherine said, drawing his attention away from me and the horse I'd mounted.

"Unbridled?" the man said, looking over at his wife. She nodded once, and he smiled, then turned to me.

"How long are you in town, Alexander?"

I hadn't booked my return flight yet, given we still had over a month before classes resumed. "That depends."

Katherine and her mother both looked at me with wide eyes, perhaps sensing my next words might be considered a bigger risk than arriving uninvited.

"On?" Mr. King prompted.

"Whether you need an extra player at the New Year Classic."

Time seemed to stand still as three of the four of us on horseback held our collective breath, awaiting Q King's response.

Finally, the man grabbed his hat and sent it flying into the air. *"Well, yeehaw!"* he shouted. "We got ourselves an attacker."

My eyes met Katherine's, and in them, I saw all I needed to. She approved. In fact, I'd go so far as to say she was impressed.

Samuel Kennedy King IV knew everything there was to know about me long before I'd arrived. I, in turn, let him know he wasn't the only one who'd done his due diligence.

"Well done, Z," said Mrs. King before she rode off, following her husband back to the barn.

I dismounted at the same time Katherine did, and we walked toward each other.

"I hope I haven't angered you."

"On the contrary. I'd say you're two for two."

I cocked my head.

"Not only did you make my Christmas wish come true, but it appears you did the same for my father. How did you know?"

"The polo community is quite small."

"He looked into you."

I held Unbridled's reins with my right hand and took hers with my left. "And I, him."

"Did you know his team lost their attacker?"

I shook my head. "Purely coincidental, in fact. At least on my part." I stopped walking, and so did she. We turned to face each other. "I'm here for you, Katherine. Only you. Say the word, and I will tell your father I'm unable to stay on."

"And break his heart? Not on your life."

"It's your heart that matters most, Katherine."

Rather than sleep, we sat by the light of the Christmas tree and talked. At the stroke of midnight, I took Katherine's hands in mine and asked her to be my wife.

While I missed the polo match, it had been with both her father's and mother's blessings. Instead, they wished us *bon voyage* on New Year's Day, when we departed on our honeymoon after marrying the night before.

6

George

They say when you meet "the one," the attraction is instantaneous. It was true for Z and me. From the first time our hands had touched in the most innocent of handshakes, desire coursed through my body. His heated eyes and the way he'd held on longer than necessary, then squeezed before letting go, told me he felt the connection as much as I did.

Every touch after that had yielded the same response. A brush of his arm or his fingertips on the small of my back when we'd exit the lift and no one was close enough to see. My nipples hardened, and I ached between my legs just by being in the same room as him.

I'd wanted Z every second of the day, waking or sleeping, for years. While I'd had an occasional dinner date, it never went beyond a quick peck on the cheek, thanking the man for a lovely time, but knowing I wouldn't see him again. I couldn't. Z was the only one I found remotely attractive, and if that meant being alone, I would.

"George? Is everything all right?" Wren whispered, then shook her head and added, "Stupid question. Of course it isn't."

What could I say? That I'd spent the last four years pining after her father? That even though we hadn't kissed a single time, I still fancied myself in love with him? "Excuse me," I muttered, getting up and racing off to the ladies' room when my eyes filled with tears.

As hard as I tried not to think the worst, my mind went there anyway. If something had happened to Z, there'd be no marriage for me, no long-term relationships of any kind. Regardless of who I met, there simply wasn't anyone on earth who could measure up to Archer "Z" Alexander.

I put my head in my hands and silently sobbed.

"George?" I heard the restroom door open and Wren say my name.

"One moment." I attempted to blow my nose as silently as I'd cried. "Apologies," I said, coming out of the stall. "He's your father, and I—"

"Stop right there. I am not entitled to be more upset than you are. No one is."

"But, we—"

"Are in love with each other," she said, interrupting me a second time.

I shook my head and half laughed. "Not in love, I'm afraid."

"Bullshit."

I raised a brow, not just at her word choice, but also the tone in which she'd said it. "Wren, Z and I aren't in a relationship. We may have flirted, but it hasn't gone beyond that."

"The two of you have been dancin' around each other for years."

I noticed she used the same expression I had.

"Even if you take the profession of everyone who works with you—meaning spies—out of the equation, anyone with eyes and ears knows how you both feel."

"We should get back to it," I said, checking the mirror and cringing at my appearance.

"God, you're so English," she muttered, following me out the door.

When we returned to the situation room, I was happy to see Nemesis and Ares had arrived. She and I cheek-kissed while Ares took his wife's coat and hung it on a hook near one of the doors.

"How are you holding up?" Nem asked Wren.

"Fine as long as I keep my brain engaged."

"Before we chart our next plan of attack, shall we address the elephant in the room, as they say?" Wilder asked when we returned to the table where he was seated.

"Which one?" Wren asked.

"Puck Lindstrom."

"Pinch and I touched on the subject briefly," I said.

"If we're looking into Seshat, we must do the same with Lindstrom," said Wren. "George, you've worked with Puck. Would you please piece together his timeline at SIS? Wild, if you would do the same with Seshat, we'll merge the two and look at how they parallel. I'll focus on Seshat's life prior to joining SIS, then I'll do the same with Puck's."

"Roger that," I said, happy to have something to do that would distract me.

"What can we do?" Nemesis asked, motioning to Ares, who stood beside her.

"While my gut is telling me Z's disappearance is somehow related to Agent Lindstrom, we should compile a list of additional suspects," Wren responded.

"Given my father's career trajectory, I anticipate it will be a long one."

"On it," said Nem. She and Ares walked over to another area in the situation room.

I focused on gathering as much information as I could about Puck. He'd joined SIS, namely Military Intelligence, Section 5, seven years ago. Z had hired him, then he was promoted at regular intervals, indicating his exemplary performance as an agent.

One of his primary responsibilities had been to hire junior agents. Of the many he had, three stood out as significant. Jamie "Beak" Thomas, Tracy "Vulcan" North, and DeDe "Seshat" Starkweather. Of them, Seshat had been an agent the longest and was also a physician's assistant.

I couldn't help but wonder how long the two had been romantic. Unlike Z and me, they wouldn't have had to hide it. Not that we *had* to hide it, either. That Z was first my boss, then my new boss' superior, was the reason we'd never acted on our attraction. As professional and responsible as Z was, he never would've crossed that line.

Were Puck and Seshat like us? Had they *known* the first time they touched? Did they look into each other's eyes and feel an immediate connection?

Given we'd learned yesterday that Seshat was working for AMPS, the human trafficking organization Puck had been investigating prior to his disappearance, it made me wonder if what was between them was real. There was a chance she'd seduced him in order to get assigned to the UK task force. And what of Puck? Was he working for AMPS now too?

I couldn't imagine anything that would compel me to abandon the oath I'd made to His Majesty the King or to his Secret Intelligence Service. Even before the training every agent went through to learn ways to prevent succumbing to the lures of our enemies, I wouldn't have been able to betray the UK.

"George and Wren? A moment?" We both stood and walked over to Pinch. "Take a look at this," he motioned to the electronic board. "This is when Z entered the vehicle, but from a different angle," he explained.

"Someone he knew was waiting for him," said Wren.

I nodded. Z's expression was one of recognition. In it, I saw more confusion than fear. "It would be logical to think it may have been Puck. Although that isn't to say so definitively."

Wren sighed and looked away from the screen. "I'm tryin' to piece together the timing of Puck's disappearance. Beak and Vulcan were killed in a shootout on the island of Gozo. How long after that took place did he go missin'?" she asked.

"According to the brief, approximately four days," I responded. "He was believed to be accompanying Cayman from Gozo to the UK, but instead, the two separated at the Malta airport."

"That was just shy of one year ago," Pinch added.

"Where in the bloody hell has the man been all this time?" Wilder said under his breath, but loud enough for everyone in the room to hear him.

Wren tapped her cheek with her index finger. "The obvious supposition is that, like his girlfriend, he went to work for AMPS." She returned to her work area. "The answer lies with Seshat. Of that, I'm certain."

Wilder made a show of cracking his knuckles. "Let's get back at it, then, shall we?"

"In the meantime, we're waiting for the NRO to supply overhead coverage along each route they may have taken from where Z's mobile was located. I'll let you know as soon as we hear anything," said Pinch, walking over to another group of agents.

"What about the car service?" I said to no one in particular. "Z hired one."

Pinch looked up. "We've contacted every one of them in London, and no one had Z's pick up on their schedule."

"Can someone check to see if he had a preferred service?" I asked.

"I'll ring Mrs. Udele," offered Wilder. The woman had once been Wilder's secretary, and until he resigned earlier today, she was Z's as well.

I glanced at the time. Twenty-three thirty. Which meant we were beyond four hours since Z got into a vehicle he'd believed would take him to my flat, then disappeared.

7

Z

"I lost touch with Seshat when we graduated from Oxford," Puck said when he returned to the room. "Two years ago, her Curriculum Vitae appeared on my desk along with several others. I interviewed her and recommended Pinch hire her. He did almost immediately. She's bloody brilliant, you know?" I caught a ghost of a smile.

"You mentioned she was."

"We were still at Oxford when I started calling her Seshat."

This was a different side of Puck than I'd seen previously. Love was reflected in his eyes as he spoke of her. "What was the significance?" I asked.

"She's the Egyptian goddess of writing, the written word, and libraries—which was where I'd always find her. I happened to be studying for an exam on gods and goddesses and stumbled on it." His eyes met mine. "The Egyptians consider the word both sacred and magical."

"She used it as her code name."

I caught another glimpse of a smile. "She did."

"You said you intended to propose at Christmas. Why didn't you?"

Puck stared at the blank wall. "After Beak and Vulcan were killed, I had to get away. I wanted DeDe to come with me, but she was needed on Gozo to help with the victims." He shook his head. "I reacted in anger, wanting her to choose. I wasn't myself. I said horrible things."

"Rather than return to Shere with Cayman, you opted to remain on Gozo?"

Puck shook his head. "I went to Malta with him first, then returned. I wanted to apologize for the way I acted…"

"What did you do instead, Sven?"

"I went to the beach. Where it happened." He leaned against the wall, then slid down it before sitting on the floor with his head in his hands. His shoulders shook with silent sobs.

Few understood the man's anguish better than I. Over the course of my career, I'd lost far too many agents. Each was a hit I still felt and always would.

Adding to my guilt was that I'd been the one to suggest Puck take over as temporary commander of the UK task force for the Gozo op. In that role, he'd recruited Beak and Vulcan. It was the first international mission either participated in, and both were killed.

Within days of their deaths, I'd recommended George be assigned to the UK task force, putting her at the same level of risk as Puck had put Beak and Vulcan. If something had happened to George because of that recommendation, I'd never forgive myself.

"Sven, I understand the guilt and anguish you feel," I said when he shook his head.

"Seshat found me there. I tried to tell her how sorry I was for what I'd said, but it was too late. She ended things with me."

"I'm sorry, Puck."

"I loved her, you know?" He walked toward the door, knocked once, then glanced over his shoulder. "Isaac or Tyra."

"Pardon?"

"The names we chose for our first child." He exited the room, and I heard the door's lock click.

Good God, had Seshat been pregnant? If so, it would go a long way to explain why Puck was so far off the rails.

I'd nearly gone that way myself when Katherine and I realized she was pregnant with our first child. Thinking back on it, she and I were practically children ourselves.

***

Katherine and I spent Christmas Eve on the sofa in front of the tree like we had each year since the night I proposed. It seemed just yesterday but a lifetime ago at the same time.

Before I'd even graduated, a friend of my parents' recommended me for a job at Military Intelligence, Section 5. As the man was a highly influential duke, the offer was immediately extended, and I accepted just as hastily.

It was no easy task to work full time and finish my studies in order to graduate and obtain my degree, but I'd managed. Credit was due almost entirely to Katherine, who made every day a joy and helped me every way she could while completing her degree at the same time.

I put my arm around her shoulders and drew her closer to me, then kissed her cheek. "It's almost midnight. Penny for your thoughts," I said.

She sighed and rested her head on my shoulder.

"Darling?" I prompted when she didn't respond.

She shifted so she faced me. "I have something to tell you, Archer."

Her frown worried me. "What is it?"

She bit her bottom lip. "I'm…um…pregnant."

"You are?" My eyes opened wide, and my grin felt as though it stretched from ear to ear.

She nodded. "I took three tests just to make sure."

I leaned forward and kissed her, then pulled back to look in her eyes. "Tell me you're happy, K."

She smiled and nodded through her tears. "I'm actually thrilled. I worried you'd think it was too soon."

"I have a well-paid job, and we've both finished our degrees. I couldn't think of a better time to start a family."

Over the course of the next eight months, my wife grew more beautiful with every passing day. We came up with lists of possible names, made decisions, then changed our minds. There was endless worrying—solely on my part—while Katherine embraced her pregnancy with grace. The other thing we changed our minds about several times was whether we wanted to know if we were having a boy or a girl. I was convinced of the latter while my bride was certain we were going to have a son.

Finally, Katherine's desire to finish decorating the nursery won out, and at our next doctor visit, we allowed him to divulge our baby's sex. We were having a boy.

We waited until the day he was born to choose his name. "Quint," said Katherine, beaming up at me as tears of joy and relief spilled over onto my cheeks.

"Samuel Quint King Alexander," I informed the woman completing the birth certificate. While he wouldn't be the fifth, we chose to honor Katherine's father in our own way.

"But we'll call him Quint," my wife repeated, gazing down at our baby boy, who appeared to like his name—and his mum—very much.

The following Christmas, we began what we jokingly referred to as our do-over. At precisely midnight, my beloved wife informed me we were once again expecting. I, of course, was absolutely over the moon about it. Not that it stopped me from fretting as much as I had with Katherine's first pregnancy.

Given the initial trimester went much the same way it had with Quint, I predicted we were having another boy. Katherine was convinced she was carrying a girl.

We'd settled on a name while it was still too early for the doctor to tell us the sex definitively. It would work either way—Kennedy King Alexander.

Our bouncing baby girl entered the world in what had to be the quickest labor on record. A mere fifteen minutes separated our arrival to the delivery room from me holding our beautiful daughter in my arms.

Both sets of grandparents were just outside the room with Quint, who I wasn't sure understood even a little what it meant to be a big brother, no matter how many times we explained it to him. However, he surprised me when my mum brought him into the room, and after taking one look at his sister, he reached out to touch her hand and said, "My baby."

As I looked into my wife's eyes, I marveled at the wonderful gifts the universe had bestowed onto us. We were madly in love, had two precious children, I had a good job where I was rising through the ranks quickly, and both sets of grandparents were healthy and happy to help out with whatever we needed.

Life couldn't be more grand, I thought to myself the day mother and newest baby were released from hospital and I parked our new car in the drive.

Both Katherine and I beamed with happiness when we walked in the front door of our recently purchased and much larger residence. It was big enough for both our children to eventually have their own room. And, as with Quint, my wife had seen to every decorating detail.

"Perfect," I said, kissing first Katherine, then Kennedy, and finally Quint. "Our life is simply perfect."

8

George

"It isn't like Mrs. Udele not to pick up," said Wilder after placing a call to Z's secretary.

"It is the middle of the night, Wild," Wren pointed out.

"In my day, those who worked at SIS were expected to answer calls regardless of the time of day or night."

Wren looked over at me and rolled her eyes. I stifled a chuckle. Wilder had been, at one time, interim director general of MI5. He'd also been offered the job of MI6 chief, which he turned down. It was his "in my day" comment that made me smile, given the man wasn't yet forty years old.

I returned to my task of piecing together the details of Puck's career and found some of the parallels to Z's interesting. Both had attended Oxford University and studied the combined major of Philosophy, Politics, and Economics, or PPE. Each had been offered jobs at MI5 prior to graduation.

The two men rose through the ranks at a similar pace, and given it was anticipated Pinch would leave his role as DG and take over as MI6 chief, it would've been a foregone conclusion that Puck would've been offered the job he was vacating.

He was given his code name after a brief stint as a professional hockey player. His father and grandfather had also played the sport at a professional level.

He'd lost his mother at a young age, and his father had passed away a year after his son started working for MI5. He had no siblings. It wasn't unusual for those like Puck and me—so-called orphans—to choose to work in intelligence. I wasn't aware of any official data on it, but I wasn't surprised when I met agents who'd lost both parents and were only children.

"I hadn't realized Puck and Seshat were at Oxford at the same time," Wren commented.

Neither had I. "Do you think they knew each other?" I asked.

Pinch looked over at me. "They did." He had a sheepish expression, as if he realized he should've shared that earlier. "I'll, um, forward the interview notes."

"Are you talking about Seshat's interview?" Wren asked, then smiled. "Never mind. You're one step ahead of me." He'd sent the same email to both of us, containing notes from his conversation with her as well as Z's with Puck.

Reading over them, nothing in particular jumped out at me as being inconsistent with what I'd learned of Puck's career. That the notes were Z's, though, almost undid me. I could hear his voice in every comment he wrote. It made sense he would've interviewed Puck. Back then, he was the head of MI5 in the same way Pinch was now.

I rested my chin in my hand. If Puck hadn't disappeared a year ago, I would've said he was one of the top agents employed by SIS. So much so, I was beginning to doubt he'd abducted Z. It just didn't make sense. Even if he'd gone to work for AMPS, like Seshat had, why Z? There were other people who made far more sense. Nemesis would've been at the top of the list, given she was the commander of the UN Coalition leading the charge against AMPS.

Any one of the task force leaders—Ares, Cayman, Poseidon, Zeppelin, or Magnet—would be next on my list of most likely to be abducted.

I stood, walked over to Pinch, and took the empty seat beside him. "Approaching five hours without a ransom request."

He nodded. "I've run down the entire list of those currently or formerly employed by SIS who are or were granted clearance above Security Check. All are present and accounted for, with the sole exception of Puck."

"If he is working for AMPS, Z makes little sense as a target."

"Agreed."

"Do you think Puck is aware Seshat is dead?" I asked.

"If he's not, his inability to make contact with her could be a motive to involve Z. Although I'd consider it a stretch."

However unlikely this theory was, if it was accurate, God knew how Puck would react once Z informed him of her demise.

"I'd suggest you get some rest, but I doubt you'd listen."

"Not a bloody chance in hell, Pinch."

"Understood."

"I feel as though I've reached a dead-end with Puck. Nothing adds up, nothing makes sense. In looking at his history, I couldn't profile him as a risk of any kind. Even with the deaths of Beak and Vulcan, his behavior—disappearing—is so out of character."

Pinch leaned back in his chair. "Agreed. However, he's our best lead at the moment. Until such time as we determine another viable suspect, receive a ransom request, or the NRO is able to track the transport vehicle, he's all we've got."

"Copy that," I muttered.

"Hey, Pinch, George, I just found something interesting on Seshat," said Wren.

"What's that?" I asked, standing to walk over to her work area.

"Not only was she born in the States, but her birth record is sealed. I'm followin' up with some of my contacts now to see if they can get me a copy." She looked at her watch. "Only eighteen thirty there. No one should be too irritated with me for callin'."

"If you don't get anywhere with your buddies, let me know, and I'll see what mine can do," Ares offered when he and Nemesis joined us.

My eyes met Pinch's. "Wouldn't her employment record indicate she was born outside the UK?"

"It would if neither of her parents were citizens. Otherwise, no."

Nemesis was standing close enough to me that when the door to the situation room opened, I felt her tense.

I was about to check who'd come in when I saw her shake her head. "What?" I whispered.

"Iris."

I could see Ares' face from where I stood, and his expression mirrored his wife's tension.

When the woman approached Pinch, Nemesis walked out of the room and I followed. Neither of us spoke until we reached the ladies' room.

"What was that about?" I asked. "Did something happen between you and Iris that I'm unaware of?" The truth was, I didn't care for her, either, but my feelings weren't strong enough that I felt it necessary to leave the room.

"Not between Iris and me, between Iris and Ares."

My brow furrowed. "I see."

"Better put, she went out of her way to make me believe they were sleeping together. She didn't stop there. According to Cayman, she also showed up in the middle of the night at the hotel room he and Ares were sharing. Scantily clad, by the way." She folded her arms and shook her head. "I know it's ridiculous that I'm reacting this way. Ares and I are married, for cripes' sake. I just don't trust her."

Not trusting a fellow agent was nothing to trifle with. Our lives were dependent on believing that every person we worked a mission with would have our backs.

"Have you talked to Pinch about this?" I asked.

Nemesis shook her head. "I've had far more important things to deal with than Iris Beachum."

"Understood. However, if her presence interferes in any way with our finding Z, I feel I must intervene."

Nem's eyes scrunched. "Wait. I recall Puck coming to her defense once or twice. Perhaps the two were also *close*."

I raised a brow. "Interesting."

"Indeed." She motioned with her head toward the door. "Let's get back in there before we miss something."

9

Z

I didn't see Puck again for several hours, and when he did enter the room, he brought what looked like a takeaway container.

"Either tell me how you expect me to help you or release me, for God's sake," I snapped, my voice tinged with irritability from lack of sleep and sustenance. However, I questioned the wisdom of allowing myself to rest or eat.

Adding to it was remembering one of the last happy Christmases Katherine and I had shared. I shook my head and looked down at the floor, recalling, as I had last night, how perfect I'd believed our life was and would continue to be. It had become everything but.

Without responding to my outburst, Puck set the tray on the floor, then approached and released my wrists. He handed me a paper cup. "It's tea."

I hesitated before taking it.

"I need your help, Z. I won't kill you unless you force me to."

"How reassuring," I muttered under my breath. Knowing it would do me no good to become dehydrated, I took a sip. He set a bag beside me. In it was an apple and two biscuits. After eating the entirety of the fruit, I felt as though my wits had been restored, at least somewhat. "Earlier, you said you intended to propose at Christmas. That was almost a year ago. What's happened since?"

He took a deep breath, looked away, and shrugged his shoulders.

"For God's sake," I repeated a second time, then raised my voice. "Fucking tell me what it is you want from me, or let me go!"

Puck scrubbed his face with his hand. "I intended to talk to her again the day everyone left for Cayman's wedding."

I took a bite of the biscuit, then put the rest back in the bag. "That is only one of many things that disappointed me. Cayman considers you to be a good friend. That you weren't at his wedding, hurt him."

"Considered. Past tense."

I felt as though I was talking to my own son, but when he was a teenager, not a thirty-three-year-old man. I cleared my throat. "Cayman *considers* you a friend.

Present tense. Although this latest stunt will certainly test the loyalty of all those who do. Myself included."

Puck looked down at the floor but, otherwise, had no reaction.

"Back to Seshat. You said you intended to contact her last Christmas. Why didn't you?"

"I watched her. She didn't seem herself."

"In what way?"

"It was almost like she was a different person."

"You're not making a bit of sense."

"This is precisely why I didn't ask for your help in a more conventional manner." He stood and paced with his hands on his hips. "I know it wasn't her, Z."

"Puck…I simply do not know what to say. I fear you're—"

Before I could finish my sentence, he stormed out of the room, leaving me to think about things I'd rather not. Namely, the Christmas after Quint turned two and Kennedy turned one.

***

"What is it?" I asked when all color left Katherine's face as she spoke to someone on the phone.

"My dad," she whispered, handing me the receiver as tears streamed down her cheeks.

"Hello?" I said, not knowing who was on the other end of the call.

"Mr. Alexander, this here's Bart Blue. I'm a hand at King Ranch. I called to let Katherine know they just took her daddy away in a helicopter, headed for the hospital in Austin. From what I heard, he had a heart attack."

"Understood. Thank you, Mr. Blue. If you hear anything else, let us know immediately."

"Yes, sir, and I'm sorry, sir."

I hung up and gathered Katherine in my arms. "Tell me what you want to do."

"We need to go to Texas. Right now, Archer."

"Understood. I'll make the arrangements."

We took the next flight out of Heathrow, but by the time we arrived, Katherine's father had passed away. Understandably, my wife was nearly inconsolable.

Three days after the funeral and church service, Katherine's mother, who insisted I call her Josephine, approached after Quint and Kennedy were asleep, asking if she could speak with me.

"Let me check on Katherine quickly." After easing into the bedroom we shared and finding her asleep, I joined her mother at the kitchen table.

"K and I spoke earlier. She doesn't want to leave."

"Leave?"

"The ranch. Texas."

I was curious about two things. First, why my wife hadn't discussed this with me. Second, how much of this was being driven by her mother. "I'll talk it over with her."

"She's afraid to tell you."

My brow furrowed. Afraid? I'd never given Katherine any cause to fear me or my reaction to something. She and I had a relationship built on mutual respect. I hadn't made a single decision that affected our lives together without discussing it with her and vice versa.

"As I said, I'll discuss this with my wife." While I tried to temper my tone, I was more abrupt than I intended to be. "My apologies. Please understand I'm not angry with you or with Katherine. There is a lot for us to discuss as a family."

When she nodded but didn't say anything else, I returned to the bedroom. I got ready for sleep as quietly as I could, then joined Katherine. When I did, she rolled her body, rested her head above my heart, and wrapped her arm around my waist.

"Apologies, I didn't wish to wake you."

"I've been dozing on and off."

She weaved her fingers in the hair covering my chest. "What's wrong?" she asked.

"Nothing that can't wait until morning," I said, knowing better than to lie to her. She picked up on even the slightest fib.

"Tell me now, Archer."

I turned my body so we were facing each other. "I've just spoken with your mum. She informed me you want to remain in Texas."

She nodded.

"Why on earth would you be afraid to discuss this with me?"

"Our life is in England. Your job. Our home."

I shook my head. "Our life is about being *together.* Wherever that may be. Nothing else matters, my darling."

Her eyes filled with tears, but she was smiling. "It means running the ranch. My mother isn't capable."

"Understood."

"Are you certain?"

"I'll ring Riv in the morning." Sir Ranald Caird, code name Rivet, was my boss at SIS. I knew him to be a family man and anticipated he'd understand why I had to resign from MI5. I wasn't proven wrong.

"If, at any time, you wish to return to the fold, so to speak, you will be welcomed with open arms," he said.

The following day, I began a new life, that of a rancher.

10

George

Pinch and Iris were still head-to-head when we returned. They'd moved to the other side of the room and were speaking in hushed tones, assumably intended to keep the conversation private.

"Nem," said Ares, approaching us. When I excused myself from their conversation and took the open seat beside Wren, she looked in Iris' direction and scowled.

"Evidently, you're aware of previous interactions," I whispered.

She leaned closer. "I've never liked her, not that I had the displeasure of havin' to work with the woman."

It was rare for a fellow agent to be so vilified and still remain in the employ of SIS. From the corner of my eye, I saw Iris put her hand on Pinch's arm. He looked down at it as if it scalded him, and he took a step back. It was impossible to gauge his annoyance from the look on his face, however. The man wore a perpetual scowl. The only exception I'd seen was when he was in the presence of his wife, Esland.

I lowered my gaze when Iris turned and walked toward me. When she passed, thankfully, and left the room, I sincerely hoped she wouldn't be returning.

Pinch made eye contact but didn't approach on his way back to his previous seat.

"Hey, Ares, I haven't received a reply regarding Seshat's birth certificate from my contacts in DC. Can you check with yours?" I heard Wren ask.

"Roger that," he responded.

As I glanced at the time, I noticed it hadn't been an hour since she made the request. However, I understood her impatience. Her father was missing, and every minute counted.

We were approaching the six-hour mark since Z was picked up by the car service. Statistically, most kidnapping victims were killed within the first three to twenty-four hours. However, this didn't feel like a simple abduction. If that had been the case, why would they have bothered stopping an hour outside the city?

"I'm having food brought in," said Wilder. "Any particular requests?"

"Thanks, but I can't eat."

"Wren said the same thing, and I'll remind you what I told her. Sustenance is vital to clear thinking. As much as rest is. Since neither of you would entertain the notion of sleep, I'll impress upon you the importance of eating."

I put my hand on my stomach. "I doubt I'll be able to keep anything down."

"Understood. I'll work out the easiest thing for your digestive system." Wilder put his hand on my shoulder. "We all know how difficult this must be for you, George."

I turned away when my eyes filled with tears. Did I truly have any business getting so emotional when Z's daughter sat a few paces from me? It felt wrong.

"I doubt you're aware he spoke with her about you. He cited wanting to pursue a relationship with you as one reason he resigned."

I didn't know what to say. It had been awkward enough discussing it with Wren when she told me Z asked her to purchase clothes for me.

"Wren was all for it, by the way. It's been a long time since Z has been happy in love. Long enough that my wife hardly remembers the relationship between her parents. At least before her mum became ill."

"We aren't in a relationship. Not yet. I believe that was the intention. However, he went missing before we had the chance for it to start."

"We're going to find him, George. We have the full force of SIS looking for him, plus the cowboy cavalry is on the way."

"The cowboy cavalry?"

"In a word, or a name, Decker Ashford. You're aware Z adopted him when he was a teenager, yes?"

"I am."

"Not only that, but it was Z who arranged for Burns Butler to mentor him."

I was astonished. "That, I hadn't known."

"Few do. In the same way you, Wren, and Quint are torn up that he's missing, Decker will be equally so."

"Of course." I leaned closer. "Do you know what's going on with Iris, by chance?"

Wilder nodded. "Apparently, she said she has information about the person who kidnapped Z."

My eyes opened wide. "That's fantastic."

"It isn't. She has stipulations."

"*Stipulations?*" I gasped.

"*Shh.* I haven't made Wren aware of what Pinch passed on to me. If I do, she'll tear Iris to shreds. Literally, I fear." He shuddered. "My wife is capable of unspeakable things, or so I've heard."

"As am I," I seethed, stalking toward the door Iris had recently exited.

The illuminated numbers above it indicated the lift was on the lowest parking level. Given it would be faster to wait than take the stairs, I tapped my foot, piecing together what I'd say to Iris once I caught up with her.

"Let her go." I spun around on Pinch, who'd walked up behind me.

"*The hell I will!*" I shouted just as the lift dinged.

Pinch put his hand on my elbow. "Hear me out. Please."

It was all I could do not to ignore him and continue my quest to find the bloody woman. "This better be good."

"Iris is helping us."

"In exchange for what?"

Pinch sighed. "That will be between her and Z."

I shook in anger. "This is bullshit."

"I would rather find him and bring him home than refuse to negotiate."

"She's one of us, Pinch. How could she do this?"

"Her motivation is in protecting someone else who is also one of us, George."

"It's Puck, isn't it? She confirmed he kidnapped Z?"

"She feels strongly that it is possible."

Feels strongly it's possible? My mind was reeling. "Why did you allow her to leave?"

"She'll be back. And when she arrives, you and Wren need to keep in mind that working *with* Iris may be the only way we can find Z." He motioned in the direction of the situation room with his head. "Come on. Wilder's ordered food."

I shook my head. "I cannot eat."

"Come on, anyway."

11

Z

Puck was in a foul mood when he returned a short while later. Like earlier, he paced. His eyes darted about, and he was sweating profusely. "Look," he finally said. "I didn't want to do this, but I've no choice."

Was this it? Did he intend to kill me because I didn't believe Seshat had somehow turned into a different person? "Do what?"

"I don't fucking care what you think, Z. What I want is help finding her. I *must* find her."

"Sven, her death was confirmed. I cannot help you find a woman who is no longer living." It occurred to me that it might be what he was asking. Did he want to see her body in order to believe it for himself?

"She isn't dead. Not Seshat. Whoever took her place is the one who's dead."

Had the man sunk into madness? If so, I had no idea how to reason with him. "I can take you to the morgue."

He swung his head back and forth as much as shook it. "You're not listening. That was not Seshat. She never would've risked the life…" He dissolved into tears, and the longer he sobbed, the more my heart broke for him.

I understood a loss so profound that carrying on seemed unimaginable. After the loss of my wife, I wondered whether I would've had the strength to go on if it weren't for my children.

***

In the year since Katherine's father passed, her mother's health had rapidly declined. I feared she wouldn't live until Christmas. Josephine's condition was also taking a heavy toll on my wife.

She'd lost a considerable amount of weight, yet any attempts I made to get her to eat resulted in her telling me she had no appetite. While she was able to keep it from me when awake, in the night, when she slept, she often groaned, bending at the waist as though she was in pain.

"Katherine, you're scaring me," I said when she sat up, turned to get out of bed, and I could see the outline of her spine.

"The kids—" she said when I put my hand around her waist, preventing her from standing.

"Are still asleep. I insist you see a doctor."

"It's just…my mom, the ranch, the kids…I'm tired. Once your parents arrive, they'll be able to help." My mum and dad had agreed to come for the holiday and would arrive in a week's time. I wished, now, I'd asked them to come sooner.

"It's more than that," I said, cupping her cheek. "Please, my darling. I beg you. Let me make an appointment for you to see someone."

"Okay," she whispered.

The soonest someone could see her was two weeks out because of the holiday. Eight days after I made the appointment, Josephine died in her sleep.

Katherine went to check on her while I looked in on the kids, who'd been sharing a room since we moved into the main ranch house permanently. No amount of coaxing could get our five-year-old son and four-year-old daughter to accept having rooms of their own.

After reassuring the kids that everything was okay—as much as I knew it wasn't—I raced down the hallway when I heard Katherine's scream followed by keening-like cries.

For the next two weeks, we stood and greeted all those who attended the visitation to pay their respects to Josephine. Followed by the funeral and burial.

In the midst of it, Katherine, my parents, and I put on a brave front to allow our children to celebrate Christmas. And, in that time, my beloved wife's health continued to deteriorate.

"Enough!" I finally bellowed when she again refused my request to reschedule the doctor appointment she'd missed.

I felt horrid when she dissolved in my arms, crying in the same way she had over her mother. I cupped her cheek, even more worried when I looked into her bloodshot eyes, the whites of which had a yellow cast to them.

"No more waiting. I'm taking you to see someone today."

I was both relieved and more worried when she didn't argue with me.

I thanked God my parents were with Quint and Wren when, after doing a rather standard-seeming examination, the emergency doctor said he wanted to admit Katherine to "take a closer look."

After several types and rounds of tests, many sleepless nights, and more tears, I sat in a room, gripping Katherine's hand in both of mine as the doctor gave us the worst news imaginable. She had advanced pancreatic cancer. At best, she had five years, even with the best treatment in the world. She lived less than one.

The first few years were the most difficult of my life. Three years after Katherine passed, I lost my mum. Two years later, my dad was gone.

I did my best to raise our two children the way I knew my late wife would have, while at the same time, caring for the ranch she'd left to them and me.

In her will, she'd requested it be renamed King-Alexander. Given there was no other family on either her mother's or father's side, there was no reason not to honor Katherine's wishes.

Shortly after her father died, I took his place at the Austin Polo Club and now, was glad I did. Riding for sport was far different than riding the ranch, and it gave me a few hours' release whenever I could fit it in, which wasn't often.

Thankfully, I had help from ranch hands who had worked for the King family like their fathers and grandfathers before them. I did my best to stay out of their way but to be available when they needed me.

Tetina Rodriguez, who we affectionately called Tee-Tee and who had worked in the dining hall kitchen since she was a teenager, kept us well-fed and was also a mother figure for Quint and Kennedy. She was kind and loving, and had known their mother well enough to share stories about her. Most were things I'd never heard, including about the year she spent as national Queen of the Rodeo during her senior year in high school.

When Quint entered junior high, he made a friend who hung out at the house with us so often that it sometimes felt as though he lived here. His name was Decker Ashford, and like Quint, he was thirteen years old.

It wasn't long before I learned why he always seemed to be at our place—the kid had been bounced around the foster care system since he was seven years old, and lately, I'd been seeing signs of abuse.

Also like Quint, Decker had lost his mum at a young age, but for an entirely different reason. From what I'd learned after contacting child protective services, both his mother and father had deserted him and, not long after, died from a drug overdose—just not together.

I made arrangements for us to be his "foster family," and after several months, I asked Quint and Kennedy, who I'd taken to calling Wren, to join me in my office. My daughter reminded me of the little bird with her abundant energy, vibrancy, and alertness. Both of Katherine's and my children were intelligent, but Wren was beyond brilliant, just like her mum.

"What did you want to talk to us about, Daddy?" Wren's voice sounded so much like Katherine's sometimes that it nearly made me weep. I missed her so.

"I'd like to run something by you. It's about Decker."

When Quint squared his shoulders, ready to defend his friend, I was proud of him. I stood, walked over, and put one arm around each of their shoulders. "I think it's time we made him a permanent part of our family, but before I do—"

Both of them were squealing with so much joy I couldn't get a word in edgewise. "Is that a yes?" I finally asked.

"Yes!" they both shouted at the top of their lungs.

"Can I tell him?" Quint asked.

I shook my head. "We need to ask him. This may not be something he wants."

"Right," Quint laughed, running from the room with Wren on his heels.

We finalized the adoption on December 23, and while Decker had spent Christmases with us before, that he was ours and we were his made it feel more magical. Long after they'd gone to bed, I sat in front of the tree like I did every year, the way Katherine and I had always done, and wished so much she was still here with me. She would've adored Deck.

12

George

My anger at Iris Beachum sent my already anxiety-ridden stress level skyrocketing. I couldn't focus on continuing my research into Puck's career or even sit still. Just sitting was too much.

We needed to find Z. *I* needed to. The longing I felt for him, to be held in his arms, to finally know what making love with him would be like, crescendoed.

I did everything I could to tamp down the idea he and I might never have the chance. I couldn't accept that possibility. As crazy as it sounded, even to me, I *loved* him. I wasn't willing to let that go.

Z was the first man, first person, who'd made me feel safe, cared for, and loved since my parents passed away within a few months of one another. My dad went first, then my mum. With her, I was sure she'd died of a broken heart.

I missed my mum and dad every day. The three of us had had such fun together. They were both gone by the time I met Z, and while my feelings for him were romantically inclined, part of me felt as though my parents had sent him to me. My own guardian angel. My heart clenched, thinking I might lose him before I'd had the chance to really know him. The way a woman knows a man. I brushed away a tear. I had to focus, had to dig deep, and figure out where Puck—who I was certain was the person in the car—would've taken him.

Blasted Iris. How could she toy with us, saying she had information, then leave? Why couldn't she share whatever it was straightaway? Especially given time was *not* on our side.

"I'm not getting anywhere with the birth certificate, either," said Ares. "It's buried deep, and I have no idea why."

"Typically, they won't release the sealed copy until both parents listed on it are dead. Even then, the person requesting it must be able to prove they are," said Wren. "At least, that's how it works in the States."

"Why?" I asked.

"To protect the biological parents' identity in the case of adoption."

"How sad," said Wilder. "But wait. If the person requesting the record doesn't know who his or her parents are, how would he or she prove they're deceased?"

"I'm not sure," Wren responded. "I've never had a reason to know." She typed several things on her keyboard. "Wait. I stand corrected. Once the adoptee reaches the age of eighteen, they can request a copy. However, it will not necessarily be released at that time." She looked at Wilder, then at me. "*Not necessarily?* That's the legal language used?" She shook her head.

"Quite honestly, I don't find Seshat remarkable enough to warrant the difficulty in obtaining her records," muttered Wilder.

"It may be that one or both of her birth parents are who's remarkable," I suggested.

Wilder's eyes lit up. "Perhaps she's the bastard offspring of a former US president."

Wren groaned. "See what I have to put up with? If there is a conspiracy to be had, my husband is ready to dive in."

He leaned down and kissed her cheek. "Our lives shall never be boring, my love."

"A true statement."

God, I envied their relationship. The ache in my chest hurt worse. I silently prayed with everything in me that we'd find Z and bring him home safely.

Wilder studied his phone. "Ah, good news. Mrs. Udele has responded. The service Z used was private. That in itself is troubling. She's passed on the number. Shall I make contact?"

I nodded when no one else responded.

At zero eight hundred, Quint Alexander and Decker Ashford arrived, along with Quint's wife, Darrow Whittaker-Alexander—an MI6 agent herself.

"We would've been here sooner, but we took Mila and the kids to Whittaker Abbey," Quint informed us.

The abbey he mentioned was the ducal estate where Wilder, Darrow, and their eldest brother, Thornton Whittaker, aka Shiver, grew up. Shiver, a former MI6 agent, now resided there with his wife and children.

"How did Wells and Huck do on the flight?" Wren asked.

"Far better than their parents managed," Darrow responded. "They do so enjoy one another's company."

From what I recalled, the two boys were quite close in age, neither yet two years old. Wren and Wilder's daughter, Katherine, was just over four months.

"Huck's never happier than when his buddy Wells is around," Decker added. He looked over at me, and I approached.

"I'm not sure if you remember me. I'm Leighton Marietta, aka George."

"Of course I remember you." Rather than shake my hand, Decker hugged me. Quint did the same, then Darrow.

Wren hugged her brother first, then Deck. "You look like shit, cowboy," she said, touching his cheek with her fingertip before looking at her brother. "So do you."

Decker's eyes closed briefly, perhaps to mask the tears that filled them. He was unsuccessful. "Let's get to work, goddammit," he muttered, then looked at his watch. "Z's been gone twelve hours, and y'all haven't found him yet? What kind of intelligence team have you assembled here?" he said to Pinch before the two men embraced.

"Best there is, now that you and Darrow joined us."

"Yeah, yeah. Give me the rundown."

I listened as Pinch and Wren briefed the three arrivals. When Wren mentioned Iris, Decker's mouth hung open.

"She's withholding information? *Where the fuck is she?*" His anger mirrored mine.

"I expect her back at any moment," said Pinch.

"She got exactly three moments before we send half of you out to get her," Decker muttered, pointing to the other MI5 agents gathered in the situation room. "What else?" he barked.

"We've been looking into another now-former agent, DeDe 'Seshat' Starkweather," said Wren. "Apparently, she and Puck—"

"Yeah, yeah," Decker repeated. "I know all this. Is there some kind of issue with 'looking into' her?"

"She was born in the States," Nemesis interjected. "We've been trying to get a copy of her birth certificate."

He scratched his head. "Trying?"

"It's sealed," said Wren.

Decker looked from her to me to Pinch. "Give me five, and you'll have it."

Wilder approached. "Sorry to interrupt. The number Mrs. Udele gave me is no longer in service."

"They went out of business overnight?" Wren gasped.

Decker leaned into me. "What are they talking about?"

"The car service Z hired."

"Fuck," he said under his breath. "They've been plannin' this for a while."

"My gut is telling me Seshat's somehow involved in this," said Wren.

Decker nodded as he typed something on his laptop. "Never ignore your gut." In less than two minutes, he announced the birth record was on its way to each of us. "Why haven't you received anything else from the NRO yet?" he demanded next.

"We're waiting," muttered Pinch.

"You Brits are too damn polite," he said, pulling out his mobile. "The clock is ticking. We don't *wait*."

While he placed a call, I pulled up the document he'd sent.

"Very interesting," Wren said under her breath.

I walked over to her and took the seat beside her. "What's that?"

"There's a recorded time of birth."

"Is that unusual?"

"Not so much unusual as what it signifies. A reported time means there was more than one birth."

"As in twins?"

Wren nodded. "Twins, triplets, etc."

"What are you thinking?" I asked.

"That we just stumbled on something very significant. Not that I know what it means yet."

"Evil twin, perhaps?" Wilder asked.

"It's been known to happen, even in the best of families," Wren responded.

"Right. Except Matthew wasn't a twin, thank God."

Three years prior, Wilder and his siblings learned their father had sired another child before he married their mother. The man had been raised by Sir Ranald Caird—former chief of MI6—and his wife, Anna, the boy's biological mother.

From what I'd heard, the man, who suffered from mental illness, took Shiver's now wife, their child, and Darrow hostage, intending to kill all of their father's descendants by way of a bomb. SIS launched a full-court press, resulting in the women and child's rescue and the arrest of the half brother. He'd subsequently been assassinated in prison. While the identity of the assassin hadn't been divulged, I'd heard a rumor that the Turkish terrorist organization Partiya Karkeren Kurdistan, or PKK, was responsible.

If that entity hadn't been dismantled via the combined efforts of the US and the UK intelligence, I would've added their leaders' names to the list of suspects in Z's kidnapping. In a briefing on terrorist organizations, he'd listed them among his mortal enemies. However, they wouldn't have taken Z hostage; they would've killed him on the spot.

"How disappointing," Wilder muttered.

I studied the name listed as DeDe Starkweather's mother—Angela Starkweather. However, under father, it said *unknown*. "How in the bloody hell did he get this so quickly?" I muttered.

When Decker shot me a look, I realized I should've kept my voice down. Wren chuckled. "If it were anyone but Decker, I'd ask the same thing. I swear the man has superpowers."

Wilder leaned back in his chair. "Aren't either of you the slightest bit curious as to who the father is?"

Wren rolled her eyes. "Whatever you come up with will be purely conjecture."

I glanced at Wren and caught her studying Decker.

"I've never seen him like this," she whispered. "I guess it isn't surprising. I don't know how his life would've turned out without Z and Quint."

"And you," her brother, who she hadn't realized was standing behind her, said. He leaned closer and spoke in a quiet tone of voice. "But I agree. Dad saw something in Deck that most people in the world would've missed, and he made sure he got everything he needed to explore his unique level of genius."

"Burns?" I asked.

"He wasn't even out of high school when Dad took him to stay with him and his wife for the summer," Wren responded.

"Deck thought our father was abandoning him. It wasn't surprising he'd think so, given both his parents had. Anyway, instead of coming straight home, Dad stayed with him until Decker finally accepted he wasn't leaving him there permanently." Quint glanced up at him. "By the way, he doesn't know Wren and I know any of this."

Whether Deck heard any of what we were saying was impossible to tell. Like Pinch, the man wore a perpetual scowl.

"Look at him tryin' to look all hardass," whispered Wren. "Quint and I know he's just a big ol' softy inside." She smiled but brushed a tear away.

"Your father is a very good man," I said, looking from her to Quint. "I know you're aware of that, but everyone who knows him thinks so."

Wren nodded. "I've been rereadin' the briefs on the Gozo ops. Losing two agents right outta the gate like that had to have been damned hard on Puck. If he is responsible for Z's disappearance, I hope he's able to help Puck."

I couldn't help but think Wren's compassion was a trait she got from her father. It was the kind of thing I'd heard Z say more than once.

"Sorry to digress, but I'm still trying to figure out how Seshat's birth record will help us find Z," said Wilder.

"I can't explain it. Like I said, it was just a feeling I had," Wren responded.

"I can," blurted Decker.

"Can what?" I asked.

"Explain how it will help us find Z."

13

When I looked up, Puck was studying me. "What were you thinking about?" he asked.

I sighed. "Losing my wife. Raising two kids on my own."

"I'm sure that was hard."

I shrugged. "Hard and yet rewarding."

"You're a good father, Z."

I raised a brow. "I cannot help but point out my children, now adults, are probably frantic with worry. I beg you to end this. Let me go."

He shook his head. "I can't. Not yet."

"Why in the bloody hell not?"

"I need to convince you Seshat is still alive."

I closed my eyes and took several deep breaths before letting them out slowly. "Get on with it, then. Why are you so intransigent in believing she wasn't the person killed two nights ago?" Something occurred to me.

When his eyes met mine, it was evident he knew what I was thinking.

He took a seat and leaned forward, resting his elbows on his knees. "Leave it alone, Z."

"The hell I will. Who is feeding you information?" I seethed.

"The person doing so is a friend who's trying to help."

"A traitor is what he is. I'll not abide this, Sven."

"She."

"Come again."

"It's a woman."

My eyes scrunched. "Someone inside SIS."

"She's trying to help," he repeated.

"You know as well as I do that sharing classified information is treasonous. There isn't a person in any intelligence agency in the world who would accept the rationale of 'she's trying to help.' Bloody fucking hell, Puck. This changes things."

He shook his head violently, like he had more than once. "You don't have a choice, Z. Why aren't you understanding? You'd rather die than help me?"

The anguish in his voice sobered me. That a man would go this far, threatening to kill another for refusing to provide the assistance he was literally begging for, woke something up inside of me.

"No, Sven. I wouldn't rather die."

His tears were different than what I'd seen previously. These were in frustration. "Just *fucking* help me."

"All right. I will."

His eyes widened. "You will?"

"This is your chance, Puck. Convince me why I should."

He stood, looking almost childlike. "I'll be back in a few minutes."

"Bring tea," I bellowed at him as he left the room. "And something more to eat."

I shook my head, wondering if I was sinking into the same madness as Puck. I, the former chief of SIS, had just agreed to help a man who'd kidnapped me. It went against every bit of training I'd ever received, every instinct—except it didn't.

I was looking at this all wrong. My instincts *were* what I was heeding. Part of me wanted to believe Puck. He was one of my agents, dammit. *I'd* hired him, not Pinch, back when I was director general of MI5.

***

"We've got this, Dad." How many times had I heard my son utter those words? If it wasn't him saying it, Decker was. It seemed every time I offered to help with something on the ranch, one of them would tell me, in so many words, that my assistance wasn't required. Quite honestly, I was getting bored.

While the time I spent in intelligence was brief, it was where my passion lay. Serving Her Majesty in SIS had been a lifelong dream, one both my parents had supported unconditionally.

I'd lived that dream for three short years. Rivet's words the day I resigned echoed in my mind often. "If, at any time, you wish to return to the fold, so to speak, you will be welcomed with open arms," he'd said.

The man was still chief of MI6. Would he recall his words? If I contacted him, would I be welcomed back? The possibility left me as excited as anxious.

Wren had left Texas to attend the University of Virginia, graduated, and was immediately offered a job opportunity by the woman who'd become her idol— Amelia "Vera" Watkins. She led one of the most elite intelligence teams in the United States. I could not be prouder of her. I was also envious.

I was a man in my early forties. While not the spry agent I once was, I still had years of service in me.

Quint, Decker, and I were seated at the kitchen table, about to finish the enchiladas Te-Te had prepared for us, when I decided to broach the subject.

"I'm considering contacting the man I worked for at SIS," I began.

Both boys, now men, looked up at me with wide eyes. "Yeah?" said Quint.

"I'm not needed around here in the way I once was. If I were to pursue this, how would the two of you feel if I returned to the UK?"

Decker sat back in his chair. "We'd miss you, but we also know you'd be doing what's right for you."

I looked at Quint, who nodded. "We get it, Dad." He scrubbed his face with his hand. "Look, I know you gave up your life in England when Wasp died and Mom wanted to return to the ranch. You could've abandoned this place and gone home yourself a long time ago, but you didn't. You knew this was the best place for Wren and me, Deck too. So you stayed. You did it for all of us and for Mom. Now, it's time you do something for yourself."

"You're sure? I could always come back—"

I stopped talking when the two burst out laughing.

Decker eventually put his hand on my shoulder. "Look, Z, we want you to be happy. I feel I can speak for Quint and Wren too when I say that's all that matters to us."

"In the same way our happiness has been all that's mattered to you," Quint added.

"I'll discuss it with your sister."

They both nodded. "Do what you want to do, but I can tell you, she'll agree with us," my son added.

My thoughts sobered. "Have I seemed that unhappy?"

"You've been treading water, Z. Bidin' your time, as they say. We've got this now. Go do you."

I smiled at Decker's phraseology. "Go do me?"

He chuckled and nodded. "Get the hell outta our hair is what I'm tryin' to say."

I put one hand on each of their shoulders. "I love you, boys."

"And we love you," said Quint.

"Ditto," added Decker.

Thirty days later, I was living in London. I'd hung onto the townhouse where Katherine and I had begun our lives together, but last year, by chance, the couple who'd been leasing it, said they were moving out. Their timing couldn't have been more serendipitous.

At first, I worried it would be too hard to live there, but given so many years had passed and necessary renovations had been performed, it didn't feel like the same place.

When I initially contacted Rivet, he invited me to dinner. "This may feel as though it's coming out of left field, but a position has just opened up that I believe you'd be well-suited for."

"Go on," I said.

"Assistant director general of MI5."

I was stunned. "I'm honored but hardly qualified, Riv."

"Nonsense. If you hadn't left all those years ago, I would've offered you the position then."

"It's been a long time since I've been in the game."

Rivet shook his head. "Intelligence isn't a game, Z. It's in your blood. Either you've got it or you don't, and you do."

"I appreciate your belief in me—"

"That's the only job on the table, Z. Take it or leave."

"I'll take it."

After the first year, I was promoted to DG. Five years later, I was named chief of MI6.

14

George

"Let me run a scenario by you," said Decker.

"Go on," said Wren.

I was about to walk away when he asked me to stay. "You're part of this," he said, motioning between himself, Quint, Wren, and Darrow. I retook my seat. He called Nemesis and Ares over, as well as Pinch.

Then he walked over to one of the electric boards, cleared the screen, and picked up a stylus. "I've heard you say all of this just in the short time I've been here."

I watched him write several things on the board, leaving room below each item.

1. Sven "Puck" Lindstrom

2. DeDe "Seshat" Starkweather

3. Puck and Seshat

4. Twin

5. Iris

6. Z

"Here's what we know. Puck has a long-standing history with MI5. He's a damned good agent and highly respected. Not to mention, Z hired him," Decker began.

"Copy that," I said when the others nodded.

"Seshat. Team player. Smart as hell, if you look at her academic record. Physician's assistant. No easy feat there. Ask Doc Butler."

"Quite honestly, I was stunned to find out it was Seshat who abducted Oleander," said Nem. "I cannot recall any occasion where I'd read someone so badly."

Decker nodded. "That's because I don't think you did."

"Sorry to interrupt," I said, half raising my hand.

"Go ahead," said Deck.

"Where is Seshat's body?"

"Here at Vauxhall Cross, in the morgue," Pinch responded.

"We should run fingerprints."

Decker smiled. "I was getting there, George, and I agree. As soon as possible."

"On it," Pinch said, getting up and walking a few paces from us. "I'm assuming we want to prove the woman killed wasn't Seshat first, then establish her identity."

"That's right," Decker told him. "While he takes care of that, let's get back to Seshat. The two most important things we learned from the birth certificate are that there were two or more births. Second, DeDe's records may have been sealed, but her mother raised her. We're waiting on the second certificate, but my guess is Angela did not raise the sibling."

"Seshat—DeDe—attended Oxford University at the same time Puck was there," said Wren, who'd stopped talking when images of Seshat and Puck appeared on another of the electronic boards. "Damn, you're good," she said to Decker.

"Taught by the best," he said, winking. "As were you."

"When this is said and done and we're enjoying Christmas dinner with Dad, err, Z, I want to know how in the hell you got your hands on all this so fast."

"Right. As if I'd tell you." He winked. "What else, Wren?" he prompted.

"Two years ago, Seshat interviewed for a job with MI5. Puck was the interviewer and recommended Pinch hire her."

Another set of images appeared on the screen. It showed the two having dinner at a London restaurant I'd heard of. It was clearly a date. "This was taken around that time."

"Were you aware of this?" Wren asked Pinch.

He shrugged. "You pay attention to the stuff that matters. At the time, it didn't."

He said something similar when I asked about Seshat's citizenship. Given agents went through multiple rounds of rigorous background checks, I supposed it made sense Pinch would concern himself with what was important rather than what wasn't.

"Who recommended Seshat for the UK task force?" Decker asked.

"Puck," Nemesis responded. "I'd also like to add that she and Puck kept things entirely professional at every stage of the mission."

Decker nodded. "Fast forward to the night Vulcan and Beak were killed."

"Cayman was pretty torn up about it, for Puck's sake especially," added Ares.

"Four days after that, Cayman boarded a plane bound for the UK. Puck was supposed to be on it, but wasn't."

"That's right," Ares responded to Decker.

"And Seshat?"

"She was responsible for caring for the rescued victims as well as supporting the familial reunification. The day after Cayman left Malta, Seshat was the one who reported Puck missing," said Nemesis.

Decker's mobile pinged. He picked it up and swiped the screen, then studied it. "This is her twin's record, and before you ask, I've confirmed Angela only gave birth to two infants." Decker's eyes widened. "*Whoa. I did not see that coming.*"

My own cell went off, and I pulled the image up on the screen. "Judee Starkweather. Fetal *death* record?" I gasped.

"Fingerprint report came back. The woman in the morgue is *not* Seshat," said Pinch.

"Figured as much." Decker stroked his beard with his hand. "That leaves us waiting on the NRO and Iris fucking Beacham."

The words had no sooner left his mouth than she walked in.

15

Z

When Puck returned, he was carrying a laptop. "The last I told you was that I'd hoped to talk to Seshat the day everyone left for Mallorca."

"Yes, for the wedding."

Puck nodded. "It was the twenty-first of December, and I was in Shere. I expected to find Seshat at the command center, but she wasn't there."

I'd ask how he knew, but I feared acknowledging again that he had someone working with him on the inside might lead to me refusing to help him once more. For now, I'd let him tell his stories and refrain from overthinking the ramifications they represented.

"I watched and waited, and two days later, she appeared. I kept my eye on her, waiting for the best opportunity to alert her of my presence, but then she did something unexpected."

"What did she do?" I asked.

"The woman exited the cottage where Seshat had been staying and followed when Oleander left the property. I shadowed them both to the house Poseidon had purchased for O and him to live in. Rather than approach Oleander, the woman remained in the trees. O must've picked up on it because she didn't get out of the vehicle. Instead, she returned to the Trace Estate."

"What happened next?"

"The woman returned as well, as did I."

I nodded, remembering the brief on what had occurred that night. As Puck said, Oleander had sensed she was being stalked. Later that night, the security on Cayman's compound was increased significantly. "Go on," I prompted.

"Given the events of the last few days, I believe her intention was to abduct O that night. Oleander, I was stunned to witness, was sloppy. Had whoever Seshat's replacement was wanted to, they could've killed her a number of times."

"What stopped her from taking O?"

"I let my presence be known. Which reminds me of another thing. The woman was not wearing NVGs."

"Were you?"

"Yes. As was Oleander."

I nodded. Why wouldn't Seshat have been wearing them? They were standard-issue.

"The woman took off through the woods. I followed and saw her get into a vehicle waiting outside the estate's perimeter. Unfortunately, my car was on the opposite side of the estate, so I had no chance of following her."

"Did you get a plate number?"

"It was a black vehicle, plates obscured, and they never turned on the lights." Puck rolled his shoulders. "I staked the place out for several days, awaiting her return."

"And?"

"She showed up on Christmas, and while she looked almost identical to Seshat, that's when I confirmed she wasn't."

"What led you to that theory?"

Puck rolled up his sleeve and showed me the tattoo on the inside of his right wrist. It was quite small, but when I leaned in, I saw it was a date. "This is the day Seshat and I met. She has an identical tattoo. The woman's wrist was bare."

"Seshat could've had it removed."

Puck shook his head. "Other things were off. Her mannerisms. Also, Seshat made an oath she took seriously. It was something she was intransigent about and refused to work for MI5 until it was guaranteed in her contract."

I nodded, remembering its entirety. "I will use my power to help the sick to the best of my ability and judgment; I will abstain from harming or wronging any man with it."

"First, do no harm," said Puck, nodding.

While I still wasn't *entirely* convinced Seshat was alive, I kept that to myself for now.

"That was almost a year ago," I prompted.

"I spent the next few months alternating between searching for Seshat and monitoring the other woman."

"Do you have any theories as to who this woman is? Or was, as it were?"

"She and Seshat look so much alike I would go so far as to say they're twins."

"This is a great deal to take in. Wait, isn't there more?" I asked when he closed his laptop.

"We'll readdress later." He stood and approached the door. "I was there two nights ago. As soon as I realized they were going to kill Oleander, I intended to act. Before I could, Poseidon and the others arrived. I would've killed her, Z, without hesitation. That's how certain I am that it wasn't Seshat pointing the gun at Oleander."

"Wait," I repeated when he was about to walk out. "The body is at the morgue. The woman's identity could easily be confirmed."

"Precisely."

"I'll need to make a call in order for that to happen. Better yet, you could release me."

"Not yet."

"Sven, why in the bloody—"

"You haven't heard the rest of the story, Z, and until I receive one final bit of information, you will not."

I wanted to roar in anger at him. Instead, I did everything I could to keep my wits about me when he left the room. It was what I'd been trained to do in order to survive any hostage situation.

I went through a training protocol once at Fort Monckton, after graduating from Oxford. The weeks I'd had to spend apart from Katherine seemed endless then. It was unfathomable to me that she'd been gone twenty-five years.

I underwent additional training when I returned to the UK from Texas and took over as assistant DG of MI5. Before I was made chief of MI6, I went through more advanced training.

***

I remained stunned that Rivet had hired me for the assistant DG job, until I met my superior. The man, Oscar Harris, had one foot in the grave, as they say. Thus, my first few weeks on the job were spent reading piles of briefs and other documents in order to familiarize myself with all the active MI5 cases.

Thankfully, Mrs. Udele, my boss' secretary, knew where virtually everything was, which meant I had to interact with the man very little.

Six months in, Rivet called me to his office. "Oscar will retire at the end of this year, and I will appoint you DG at that time."

I gave him no argument. When that day arrived, I promoted another MI5 agent to take my place as assistant.

Three years later, that man—Jasper Torosyan, code name Pimm—changed my life.

"Z, I'd like you to meet our newest agent, Leighton Marietta," he said, approaching me in the hallway just outside my office.

When she put her hand in mine, I felt a surge of energy course through my body. I stared into her eyes, knowing I hadn't met her previously but feeling a connection so strong it couldn't be denied. I didn't want to let go. It was madness that I wanted to pull her into my arms instead. Before I released her, I squeezed her hand and her cheeks flushed.

Jasper cleared his throat. "Agent Marietta comes to us fresh out of Monkton; however, she's yet to be given a code name."

"Did you say Marietta?" asked Wilder, walking up to us. When he introduced himself to Leighton and touched her, I could feel a growl forming in my chest. "What about Georgia?" he suggested.

I hated it on the spot. No one suggested a code name for a person they didn't know. The woman disengaged her hand from his by shrugging. "It's fine," she said.

"Georgia it is," proclaimed Wilder, puffing out his chest and taking her hand in his a second time.

When Leighton's eyes met mine again, I realized I was behaving just like Wilder. Or I wanted to. What was I thinking? The woman had to be twenty years my junior, not to mention, she was now one of *my* agents. Pimm may have hired her, but I was her boss, for God's sake.

"If you'll excuse me." I glanced at her once more. "Welcome aboard, Agent Marietta." Even when I walked away, I could feel her eyes following me.

Lord, help me. I'd met a woman whose mere presence affected me in ways no other had since Katherine, and there was absolutely no way I could pursue a relationship with her.

I returned to my office, shut the door—perhaps a little too forcefully—and plopped in my chair. There'd been many times in my life when I'd questioned the existence of God or some other higher power. Now, I cursed him.

My wife had been gone twenty years. Her death had devastated me. I was twenty-seven years old, hardly even a man, when she passed away. I'd lived every year since as a veritable monk. I'd raised my children in a place utterly foreign to me until they no longer needed my guidance.

And how was I to be rewarded? By having the only woman who stirred something in me in all that time be untouchable.

I rested against the back of my chair and closed my eyes. While I'd never believed I was entitled to a better life than anyone else, I was beginning to resent that mine seemed so much worse.

16

George

I was overwhelmed by everything that happened seemingly simultaneously. The medical examiner confirmed the woman in the morgue was not Seshat. While the news wasn't surprising, what it meant was mind-boggling.

And, while I was anxious to learn if the NRO had found any other footage of the vehicle Z was transported in, I was torn between reviewing the information they'd just sent and hearing what Iris had to say.

Decker and Pinch moved to the other side of the room, essentially ignoring Iris, and I followed. I leaned in when they accessed what was sent by the NRO.

"Reconnaissance believes they picked them up on M1 and A-45," Pinch said in a hushed voice. "Bloody black sedans," he muttered. "That's what took them so long."

Wren's ears pricked up, and she joined us. "Final destination?"

Pinch's eyes met hers, and he put one finger in front of his mouth, then looked in Iris' direction. It didn't appear she was paying attention. That didn't mean she wasn't.

"They're working on it. Apparently, the driver went underground at some point," Pinch said barely above a whisper.

"Underground?"

"These bastards know what they're doing," added Decker. "Fucking assholes."

"The last pinned location is in Northampton, and that's what makes it difficult. The area dedicated to industrial complexes is at least half or more of the entire city, most of which have interconnecting underground tunnels for loading and receiving. The NRO was able to determine which tunnel they accessed, which does give us something to go on, but it's still tantamount to finding a needle in a haystack, as they say."

"Let's see what she's got." Decker motioned to Iris, and Pinch nodded.

"What took you so long?" Pinch seethed as he approached the already flustered-looking woman.

When Decker joined him, his penetrating scowl matched Pinch's.

"It took me a while to find what I was looking for. Two things, actually. For one, it required I wait until this morning."

"Jesus Christ," barked Decker. "Just get to the fucking point."

"Not until you agree to my conditions—in writing."

It was a toss-up as to who would throttle Iris first. I'd have a go at it, but it appeared either man standing in front of her would beat me to it.

Decker leaned forward, close enough that his nose was almost touching hers. "Hand…it…over."

Iris stood her ground. Her only movement was to glance at Pinch.

"As I told you previously, what you're requesting can only be approved by Z."

"Bullshit. Z is no longer chief of MI6. You are in the interim."

I had to give it to the woman. As intimidating as he and Decker were, I wasn't sure I'd be able to deny them.

"Here's what I'll agree to. If what you give us results in Z's rescue and his safe return, meaning alive, then I'll take it under consideration."

Decker turned and glared at him. "What does she want?"

"Immunity," Iris responded before Pinch could.

"From?"

While Decker asked the question, her gaze remained fixed on Pinch.

"Passing on classified information."

I swear it looked like there was smoke coming out of Decker's nostrils. "To whom?"

"Puck," said Iris.

From the corner of my eye, I saw Wilder put his arm around Wren's waist, preventing her from getting any closer to Iris and the two men.

"Technically, he's still an SIS agent as well as a member of the UK task force," said Nemesis. "Given that, as long as whatever Iris passed along was not something that would compromise the safety of the UK and its citizens or affect the mission of the UN Coalition Against Human Trafficking, I can make the deal."

I wasn't sure who was more stunned—Iris or Nem's husband. I wasn't far behind them.

When Ares approached, Nemesis squared her shoulders. "I cannot speak for the rest of you, but in my opinion, what she's asking will be worth it if it means we find Z."

Pinch nodded. "Agreed."

"We've no time to waste. I'll draft the offer, and Iris and I will sign it."

"Nem?" I heard Wren say. "Are you sure about this?"

"As I said, as long as whatever she's shared does not compromise the safety of the UK or the mission, I am absolutely certain."

Wren nodded, and Nem walked over to her laptop.

I turned back to Iris. The look on Decker's face and how close it remained to Iris' reminded me of the movie where a threatening—perhaps terrifying wouldn't be too strong of a word—extraterrestrial breathed down the neck of a female warrant officer.

"I've digitally signed the document. Your turn, Iris."

The woman glanced over her shoulder as if she was determining who posed a greater threat—Nem or Decker. Rather than wait, Nemesis stood and carried the laptop over to her.

"Sign it," she spat, setting it on the nearest table.

The situation room was as quiet as I imagined it would be if those in the room were watching an op where our greatest enemy was about to be taken out.

Iris added her signature via her SIS logon, then turned to face those of us gathered.

"Puck received a message from Seshat via the secure portal." She cleared her throat. "In terms of what it said, I only know what Puck shared with me."

"Which was?" Decker growled.

"She said she was forced to leave the UK and go into hiding."

"This is ridiculous," I said under my breath. "This is what we've been waiting for? This is what you hoped would assure your immunity?" My voice grew louder with every word I spoke.

"There was more. She said the reason she had to leave England was because she was pregnant and feared for her life and that of her child. Puck's child."

I was stunned, as it appeared everyone else in the room was. Supposing it was true, no wonder he went off the rails.

Pinch was the first to speak. "When did he receive it?"

"The day before yesterday."

"Is he aware Seshat was shot?" I asked.

"Yes."

"Because you told him?"

"No."

"How was he made aware?"

Iris' eyes met mine. "He was there."

"You said there were two things. What was the other?" Nemesis asked.

Iris hesitated, and I nearly came out of my skin when Decker's fist connected with the table next to her. More startling was when he pulled out his firearm and aimed it at her.

"Stop this cat-and-mouse bullshit!" he bellowed. "If you've wasted all this time, making us believe you have information that would help us find Z and don't, I swear to fucking God I will kill you."

Like before, everyone in the room froze.

"Do not move!" he shouted when she appeared she might. "Tell me what else you've got."

"It's a lease agreement in Puck's name for a warehouse in Northampton. I believe that's where he's taken Z."

I expected *someone* to issue a command for us to deploy or, at the very least, say *something*. Decker, however, was studying his mobile, and his brow was furrowed.

"Deck?" Nem prompted.

"Hold up," he said, looking over at Pinch. "Have someone take her into custody. Make sure she has no access to communication."

"What?" Iris screeched. "We had a deal. Nemesis signed it."

"There were two parts to that deal. First, you'd be given immunity *after* Nemesis reviews everything you passed on and to whom. Second, the information you gave us has to result in Z's rescue and safe return. No one said anything about not lockin' you up in the meantime."

"But—"

"Get her out of here, boys," he said to the two MI5 agents Pinch had called over.

"You were looking at something on your mobile. What's happened?" I asked Decker once Iris had been taken from the room.

"I didn't want to say anything in front of Beachum, but I may have a lead on Seshat's whereabouts."

My eyes opened wide.

"Right now, though, we need to go get Z." His eyes met Nem's, and she nodded.

"All right, everyone, let's suit up and move out. The location is over an hour's drive, so Pinch, Decker, and I will craft a plan on the way."

17

Z

I got relatively good at marking time, although sometimes my mind wandered. I attributed my failure to maintain what I considered my normal focus to my lack of sleep.

My best guess was that it had been two hours since the last time Puck walked out.

Over the course of the last several hours, he'd looked increasingly haggard. More like a man nearing the end of his rope. I vacillated between thinking he was mad and wanting to believe him.

What I was most curious about was the timing of my abduction. It couldn't have been my resignation. That alone made little difference. He'd be prosecuted for kidnapping either way. Which meant something had to have happened. The only thing that made sense was Seshat's death.

Is that what had led him to think he had no hope? But wouldn't he have just given up rather than take me hostage? I couldn't make sense of any of it.

I ran my hand through my hair, knowing I desperately needed a shower and thankful the bathroom he periodically led me to—upon my request—had a toilet and sink but no mirror. Not that I was vain.

Until I'd met George, that is. Regardless of the number of times I told myself we couldn't be together romantically, it didn't alter the fact that I found myself stopping in the men's room at Vauxhall Cross to check my appearance prior to going into any meeting where she'd be present.

Thinking about it now, I realized my desire, my longing for her, had never diminished. I'd just allowed my stubbornness to overwhelm it.

When I'd finally pulled my head out of my arse and done what I should've months, if not years, ago, here I was, kidnapped on the very night I planned to spend with her in my arms.

Lying on this cot, not knowing what Puck intended or even his current mental state, forced me to acknowledge the possibility I may never see her again.

I'd wasted four years, putting my job before my *life*. Now, fearing the end might be approaching sooner than I'd hoped, I saw the absolute stupidity in my actions. Would that I could go back and do it all differently.

Between the time I met George and now, there'd been an endless upheaval at SIS, starting with Rivet's forced retirement due to a family scandal so far-reaching, if he hadn't, the outcome might've put the entirety of MI6 in jeopardy.

Upon his departure, the UK Foreign and Commonwealth Development Secretary had offered the chief's position to Thornton "Shiver" Whittaker. Since he wanted no part of it, his brother, Sutton "Wilder" Whittaker, was offered the opportunity. When he turned it down, I'd visited the secretary's office and pleaded my case for why I should be promoted to the job.

Whether my rationale had been compelling or the man was just grateful to find someone willing to take on the role, I'd never know.

Looking back, I couldn't remember why it was so important to me. Why had I thought the appointment would make up for everything else lacking in my life? Mainly, romantic love.

Had I truly believed Katherine was it for me? That I'd never experience companionship again? I hadn't even tried. Better put, I'd done the opposite. I'd essentially pushed the possibility away.

From the moment my eyes met Leighton "George" Marietta's, I thought about it—her—constantly. I'd been in a heated argument with myself for four bloody years. It seemed ridiculous, reflecting on all the nights I wouldn't have gone to bed alone. All the mornings I could've woken up with George in my arms. The countless hours she and I could've spent making love. For what? A fancy office? A title that made me an administrator rather than allowed me to do what I'd always enjoyed more than anything else professionally—investigating.

I'd dedicated a great deal of time in the last few months to the UN Coalition Against Human Trafficking, an organization for which I served in a purely advisory role. Instead, I'd suited up and pushed my way into ops no one had assigned to me. Subsequently, I'd felt more alive than I had in years.

Perhaps that was why I'd finally woken up and made the decision to resign as chief. The irony that I had and still didn't know how it felt to hold George in my arms, kiss her, and make love to her ate away at me.

And what about her? She'd not kept her attraction to me a secret, nor had she dated much in the time I'd known her. That in itself was a tragedy. Had she waited for me, foregoing another chance at happiness, only to have what might have been between us end before it could begin?

It wasn't just George that Puck was keeping me from. I had a brilliant and beautiful daughter, two amazing sons, a son-in-law, two daughters-in-law, and three grandchildren. Huck, Decker and Mila's son, was the oldest and would be two at the first of the year. Wells, Quint and Darrow's son, was two months younger than his cousin. Katherine, my only granddaughter, was approaching four months old. We'd already planned to spend Christmas together at the ranch in Texas. Would I be alive to spend it with them? The idea I wouldn't nearly had me in tears of frustration and anger.

When I heard the doorknob jostle, I tamped down the building rage I felt. If I had any hope of getting Puck to let me go, I had to convince him it was in his best interest to do so. I had no means to force him.

"You look like hell," I blurted when the door closed behind him. "So much for the kind-and-gentle approach," I thought, looking into his eyes.

"You would too if you were me," he mumbled.

"Why are you doing this, Puck? What purpose does kidnapping me serve? You had to have had a game plan when you set all this in motion."

"I've told you time and again that I want your help finding Seshat."

I shook my head. "And as I've said time and again, you could've just come to me and asked."

He studied me, one brow raised. "Could I have? And you would've done what? Exactly as you have done?"

"I cannot say, given you never allowed me the opportunity."

"That's bullshit, and you know it. You would've insisted the deaths of Beak and Vulcan had sent me over the edge, most likely recommended therapy. If I, in turn, insisted the woman at the command center in Shere was not Seshat, you probably would've sent me to the loony bin straightaway, particularly after the imposter convinced you I was mad."

"Puck—"

"Can you honestly tell me you and the rest of the teams haven't come to that conclusion anyway? That I've gone off the rails and that was why I disappeared?"

"I cannot."

"When the imposter abducted Oleander, would you have looked at me as an accomplice?"

I shook my head. "I cannot say definitively."

He looked down at the floor. "Tell me it hasn't crossed your mind."

"I cannot," I repeated.

"I *kidnapped* you, and yet your every thought is that I'm delusional. You haven't even entertained the idea that everything I've told you is true, but you want me to naively believe that all I had to do was *ask* for help."

I had nothing to say. Quite frankly, he was more lucid than I'd seen him thus far. He was also right. No one would've taken him seriously. No one would've listened. We *would* have arranged for psychiatric care. We would not have believed his claim that the woman on the UK task force was an imposter. Nor would we have acted on it. "Where do we go from here?" I finally asked.

"First, you give me your solemn vow I will not be prosecuted for abducting you. Second, you will back an investigation into Seshat's disappearance with the full force of SIS."

Apparently, whoever was feeding him information hadn't informed him of my change in status. "While I'll do what I can, I am no longer chief of MI6." Based on his reaction, I was right in thinking he hadn't been made aware. Before he could respond, his mobile vibrated.

Puck walked to the opposite side of the room and swiped the screen. His eyes widened. "I *knew* it. Fingerprints have confirmed the body in the morgue is not Seshat."

I was about to ask who he'd received the information from, but stopped myself when his entire demeanor changed and he returned to the chair. He stuffed his mobile in his pocket and leaned forward, resting his elbows on his knees. "There's more. I told you I was there when Oleander was rescued."

"I recall."

"I received a message from Seshat the day before it went down." He took a deep breath and scrubbed his face with his hand. "She said she left England because she feared for her life as well as that of our child."

"Your child?"

"Apparently, Seshat learned she was pregnant after I disappeared. It's one of the reasons I started tracking the imposter again that afternoon."

It was enough on its own that Seshat was missing and perhaps in danger. Adding a child to the scenario went a long way to explain Puck's state of mind.

"You said you just received the message two days ago? Why did she wait so long to contact you?"

"I don't know, Z, but there's proof now that it *wasn't* Seshat who abducted Oleander. Whoever it was, was working for AMPS."

"You said she looked nearly identical."

He nodded.

"Does Seshat have a sister?"

"Not that I'm aware of."

I closed my eyes and took a deep breath. Better put, a leap of faith. "You said in order to let me go, you wanted my vow you'd not be prosecuted and that an investigation into Seshat's disappearance would be backed by the full force of SIS."

"Yes."

"You've got it. Even if it means I have to be reinstated at MI6."

Puck smiled. A genuine smile. It was the first I'd seen since Beak and Vulcan were killed. He stood and put his hand on my shoulder. "Thank you."

Just as he released the ties binding my wrists, the building's alarms went off. He raced out of the room and through the door, pulling it closed behind him.

Seconds later came the sounds of muffled shouting too far away for me to ascertain what was being said.

I'd rarely been a praying man, at least for myself. For Katherine, Quint, Wren, and Decker, I'd said many. Also for the agents and operatives I oversaw.

Today's prayer was for me—and for Puck. I looked up at the ceiling, then closed my eyes. "Please, God, I beg you. Whatever is happening on the other side of that locked door, let us walk out of here alive."

Wait! I hadn't heard the lock click! I rushed over and grabbed the handle. When it unlatched, I raced out of the room.

18

George

It would be impossible for me to count the number of ops I'd been on in the course of my career as an agent. It didn't matter if it were a thousand before or a thousand that would come after; this one was different. This one was personal. More than that. *My* life depended on it.

I was thirty-four years old and had never experienced the love of a man like I knew deep in my soul I would with Z. He and I were meant to be together, and if Puck had done anything to keep that from happening, I'd not think twice about killing him.

I looked out the window of the SUV, wishing we were being transported via helicopter instead. We were almost two hours away from where Z was being held.

That we'd arrive in the middle of the workday was to our advantage. We were able to get a read on the location of the warehouse Puck had rented via the NRO overheads. While it was in an older development, many of the buildings in its immediate vicinity were quite busy. And that meant noise. A lot of noise. Not only that, but big trucks parked there would allow us to avoid any cameras Puck may have set up.

Wren, who was seated beside me, reached over, took my hand, and squeezed my fingers. "Not much longer."

I'd say five minutes would be too long a time to wait. However, she had to be just as anxious. Probably more so.

I closed my eyes for several seconds, reminding myself I couldn't think about Z as the man I loved. I had to think of him as a hostage who it was our mission to rescue.

After taking several deep breaths, I opened them to review the plan Nem, Decker, and Pinch had crafted and forwarded to each of us. They'd determined entry points based on the building's schematic and divided us into teams. I was assigned to the second unit to enter the building.

We arrived one hour and forty-five minutes after we left Vauxhall Cross—slightly over eighteen hours after Z was abducted. If this were any other kidnapping, time would be against us. Our window was rapidly closing, at least statistically speaking. However, there was nothing textbook about what we were dealing with. My biggest concern going in was Puck's state of mind as well as his level of desperation. I truly didn't think he'd harm Z, at least not intentionally.

I watched as Pinch's team, who occupied the first SUV to pull in, exited the vehicle. It was their job to confirm the points of entry as well as determine how many people were in the building along with where they were located.

I listened through the comms as each member of the team validated their positions, then I heard the one vital piece of information I'd been waiting for.

"Two people confirmed inside, close proximity to one another," said Pinch.

I checked my mobile as what was indicated on the Doppler device was superimposed on the building's schematic. It showed two people inside a storage room.

"Wait for my count," Pinch commanded. Several minutes felt like hours before I heard the sound of someone kicking in a door, followed by the building's alarm going off. The image on my mobile immediately changed, indicating the movement of one person exiting the room.

When Pinch announced we'd deploy on his count of three, I exited the SUV and assumed the position I'd been assigned.

We stormed the building, and the first thing I saw was Puck standing with his arms in the air. Seconds later, I heard the one voice I prayed I would.

"Stand down! Stand down!" Z shouted, coming out a door, waving his hands in the air.

"Z!" I said, pulling off my helmet and racing toward him as he ran to me. "Thank God you're all right. Thank God, thank God," I repeated as tears streamed down my face.

His eyes bored into mine, and he cupped my cheek. "I should never have waited to say this. I love you, George. I love you so much," he said right before his mouth crashed into mine.

I heard others shouting behind me, but their words didn't register. I'd waited my whole life for this kiss, and I refused to pull away before Z did.

He didn't until we heard Wren's voice shout, "Daddy!"

I stepped back, giving them space to embrace. Quint was right behind her, and as the two men hugged,

Decker approached. He tore his helmet from his head and tossed it on the ground, then entered Z's open arms.

While I'd heard both Wren and Quint tell their father how much they loved him, it wasn't until I heard Decker say, "I love you, Dad," that I broke down.

I bent at the waist as sobs of relief racked my body. When I felt a hand on my back, I stood up and looked into Z's eyes. "I love you," I whispered. "And I'm never letting you out of my sight again."

He smiled and caressed my face with his fingertips. "Nor I, you."

Z looked over at Puck, and his brow furrowed. He turned toward Decker. "Release him."

Decker's eyes scrunched. "But—"

"I said to release him."

"Don't, Z," I heard Puck tell him. "Let them take me in."

What I saw next nearly leveled me. Z walked over to where Puck stood, handcuffed, with his head down. The man who'd captured my heart the very moment our eyes first met put his arms around the person who I'd feared had taken him from my life, and embraced him. He continued to hold him as Puck wept on his shoulder.

"Uncuff him. Now!" I heard Z shout at Pinch several seconds later. Unlike Decker, he immediately followed Z's orders.

After he had, Puck raised his head. I held my breath, not having any idea what would happen next.

"Sir, you need to let them—"

He leveled his gaze at Puck, rendering him silent. "We'll brief Pinch on our discussions upon our return to London."

Wren approached him. "Dad? What are you doing?"

Ignoring her, he put his hand on Puck's shoulder. "Am I making myself clear?"

Decker took a couple of steps toward them. "Z, we should have a medic check you out."

"Absolutely not. We're going home," he responded, walking toward the open warehouse door. "Now!" he added when no one else moved.

Once outside, I offered to ride in one of the other SUVs to give Wren, Quint, and Decker time with their father, but Z wouldn't hear of it. "Not letting you out of my sight, remember?"

He sat between Wren and me on the second-row bench seat and held each of our hands but didn't speak.

No one did until Decker pulled up in front of his town-house and parked.

"Please understand I know what I'm doing. Do not question it or go against me." He looked first at Decker, then at Quint, who was in the front passenger seat, then at Wren. "Do I have your agreement?"

It took a few seconds before any of them spoke. "You've got it, Dad," said Quint.

"I'm not in favor of this, but okay, Dad," said Wren.

The four of us waited for Decker's response. I couldn't speak for anyone else, but I was holding my breath.

"I need an explanation," he said.

"And you'll get it. For now, give me your word."

Decker shook his head and peered into Z's eyes. "You have my word, but like Wren, I'm not in favor of it."

As we walked to the door, Z took my hand in his. "While we wait for the others, I'm going to shower and change."

"I should probably head to my flat and do the same. Wait…"

He raised a brow.

"Um, Wren said there were clothes here."

His eyes twinkled. "That's right. There are." He turned to Wren, Quint, and Decker. "If you'll excuse us, we'll be down in a few minutes."

He took my hand and led me upstairs without waiting for a response.

19

Z

It had been a very long time since I seduced a woman. Not so long since I'd fantasized about it, though. Given I'd hoped George would come home with me after our date, I'd already prepared the place for romance. There were candles and flowers in the bedroom and bathroom, even something for her to wear on our "morning after" if she didn't want to return to her place in what she'd worn to dinner. There was also something for her to snuggle up in at the breakfast table.

Shortly after I resigned, I'd placed a call to my daughter. "Wren, I know this conversation may be slightly uncomfortable for you," I began after I told her I was leaving MI6. "However, I need your help, and I've no one else to ask."

"Of course. Anything. You know that."

"I need you to purchase clothing for a woman and deliver what you pick up to the townhouse."

Our already ridiculously uncomfortable—for me, anyway—conversation became much worse when my daughter burst out laughing. She may have even snorted.

"They're not for me," I said when I realized how what I said must've sounded.

"I know. Sorry." She gasped between hiccuping laughter.

"It's, um, for George."

She caught her breath and cleared her throat. "That's what I figured."

"And you found it uproarious?"

"No. Again, sorry. It's just…I'm happy for you, Dad. I mean that sincerely."

"I hope you know this doesn't change the way I felt for your mother—"

"Z, stop. Mom passed away twenty-five years ago. I would never begrudge you a relationship with another woman, and neither would Quint. We want you to be happy," she'd said right before our call ended.

While I was thankful my daughter had done as I asked, it occurred to me George might find it curious. I stopped when we reached the top of the stairs.

"Um, George, err, Leighton, there's something I need to explain."

"Go on."

"It may have been presumptuous of me, but I asked Wren…God, I'm making a mess of this, aren't I?"

She laughed. "First, as I said, Wren already told me about the, um, favor you asked of her. Second, you can call me George. It doesn't bother me. I've grown accustomed to it. In fact, I like the way it sounds when you say it."

Remembering how she'd gotten the code name made me frown. "Wilder suggested it."

"He did not. He suggested Georgia. You're the one who shortened it to George."

"I did?"

She smiled and nodded.

"As for the *favor*, I hope you don't think I was being presumptuous." I felt my cheeks flush.

"Don't be embarrassed. I thought it was sweet."

"You did?"

"Very. Now, are we up here to 'freshen up,' or was there something else you had in mind?"

I wrapped my arm around her and pulled her body tight to mine. "I have so many things in mind." I let one hand drift down to her bottom. "God, I love your arse. Do you know how long I've wanted to do this?"

She reached around and put her hand in the same place mine rested on hers. "Probably as long as I've wanted to."

"George, I—"

"Z, forgive me, but the others are arriving soon…"

"Right." Again, I was making a mess of this. "There's one more thing I need to ask."

"Yes?"

"Once everyone has gone, will you stay?"

She leaned up and kissed me, then repeated my words back to me. "Not letting you out of my sight, remember?"

I led her to the guest room where Wren had left the purchases I'd asked her to make, then showed her the door that led to a private guest bathroom.

After she thanked me, I walked across the hall and into my room, where vases of flowers I'd picked up on my way home yesterday still looked as fresh and lovely as they had what seemed a lifetime ago.

If only my children weren't downstairs, waiting for me, George and I would be in this room together like I'd so often dreamed of. For now, though, the quicker I showered, changed, and returned downstairs, the sooner we could be done with the meeting I planned. Then George and I would have days—no—a lifetime of being together.

As I exited the bedroom, she came out of the guest room. "Perfect timing," I said, holding my arm out to her.

Her hair was wet but up, albeit a little messy and sexy as hell. The cream-colored knit outfit she wore hugged her curves perfectly.

"You look gorgeous, by the way."

"Thank you. As you know, Wren chose what I'm wearing. Including the, um, sexy undergarments."

I stopped walking, pulled her against me, and rested my hand on her behind. "The minute we are alone, know that the first thing I will want to see are those sexy undergarments."

She wriggled out of my grasp but looked over her shoulder as she walked away. "Yes, sir," she murmured,

winking and making it nearly impossible for me to follow her downstairs.

Just as I reached the bottom step, there was a knock
at the door. "Cayman? What are you doing here?" I
asked when I opened it and saw him standing there.

"May I come in?"

"Yes, of course. My apologies. I thought you and
Bexli were in Mallorca."

"We cut the trip short after I heard what happened.
How's Puck?"

I looked over my shoulder to the drawing room
where he stood. After taking Cayman's coat and hanging it on the rack near the door, I waved him inside.
"See for yourself."

"He's here?"

I lowered my voice. "He is, and in a few minutes,
that he is will make more sense."

"Hello again." I leaned in to kiss George on my way
in. "Has everyone arrived?"

"Yes, I believe so. I didn't expect to see Cayman. I
thought he was on holiday."

I followed her gaze to Puck and him. "He cut it short when he heard what happened." I kissed her once more, then asked if I could have everyone's attention.

"Thank you for meeting me." I looked around the room. Wren, Quint, Decker, and Puck were here, as were Pinch, Nemesis, Ares, and Wilder. "I believe we're all present." I turned to Cayman. "Thank you for joining us."

He nodded.

"I'll keep this brief as I know, like me, most of you didn't get much rest last night."

"Z, before you begin, may I speak?" Puck asked.

"You may not." I cleared my throat. "To begin, the events of the last twenty-four hours were not quite as they seemed. Further to that, while many in this room believed Agent Lindstrom was missing, he has, in fact, been working undercover for the last several months."

From the corner of my eye, I saw Nemesis raise a brow. However, thankfully, she didn't challenge me.

"A brief will follow in the next few days that will explain more, but, in the meantime, I am requesting SIS take on a newly crafted mission." I looked over at

Pinch. "As you are interim chief, I'm asking for MI6's support specifically, as well as that of MI5."

His eyes were scrunched, but he nodded. "Yes, sir."

Next, I turned to Nemesis. "This new mission will also involve the UN coalition as well as the five task forces. In fact, I predict it will ultimately fall under your jurisdiction."

Like Pinch, she gave me a look. Also like him, she verbalized her support.

"Very good. If the rest of you could bear with me another few minutes, I'd like to speak with Puck, Cayman, Nemesis, and Pinch privately."

I was about to lead them into my home office when Decker approached.

"Go ahead," I said to the others. "Yes, Deck?"

"I received information earlier today that may prove useful to the mission."

I studied him for several seconds.

"Look, I gave you my word."

"All right. Come on." I motioned him through the door, but before following, I returned to George. "This won't take long, I promise."

"Take all the time you need, Z. I'm not going anywhere."

"I cannot tell you how happy that makes me." I kissed her once more, then joined the others.

"My official statement is, given Puck was undercover, we arranged to meet in Northampton. Any questions?" I glanced around the room, challenging everyone in it, Puck included, to speak.

"Excellent," I said when no one did. "Now, I will let Agent Lindstrom brief you in detail; however, know that there is a tremendous sense of urgency involved. It is our belief an imposter has infiltrated the UN coalition's command center in Shere. You'll need to assign teams to assess damage control."

"Roger that," said Nemesis.

"While we've yet to confirm the identity of the imposter—" I stopped talking when Pinch raised his hand. "Yes?"

"I believe we have confirmed her identity."

"Excellent," I repeated. "You, Puck, and Cayman can prepare the brief."

I folded my arms when no one in the room responded. "I'll remind you all that I am no longer employed by

SIS, effective a little more than twenty-four hours ago. As such, I should not be privy to any further information regarding this mission."

Nemesis stood. "Z—"

I raised my hand. "In other words, I am taking some much-deserved time off. As is Agent Marietta."

"Also no longer employed by SIS," said Pinch, winking.

I raised a brow, then turned to Decker. "Whatever information you have, you may share directly with the rest of those in the room. Now, if you'll excuse us, I need a few minutes alone with Cayman and Puck, then you may all take your leave."

I waited for the others to exit the room, then closed the door behind them.

"Before you say anything, Puck, I gave you my word and I will not go back on it. Nor will I allow you to do the same."

Without allowing him time to respond, I addressed Cayman. "While I am in no position to issue an order, I would like to suggest Puck be in charge of the new mission with you as his second."

"Understood, sir."

"That will be all."

I stopped Puck on his way out and offered my hand. Rather than shake it, he embraced me, then stepped back.

"I don't know what to say, sir."

I put my hand on his shoulder. "If you need anything, no matter what it is, contact me and I'll do everything in my power to see that you get the help you require. I may even go a bit beyond my power, as you witnessed this evening." I smiled and winked.

His eyes scrunched. "Why are you doing this?"

"Easy answer. Because you're one of mine and I let you down. Good night, Puck."

I stood by the door, ushering everyone out. When Wren, Wilder, Quint, and Decker were all who remained, other than George, I closed the door and returned to the main room, where they waited.

"You four, along with Mila, Darrow, Huck, Wells, and Katherine, are my family, and I love you."

"We love you, Z," said Wren.

I smiled at my daughter. "As such, I'm asking you all to understand I need some time." I turned to George and held out my hand. "We need some time," I added when she took it.

Wren stood. "I can't speak for anyone else, but given it's something you've never asked of us before, I think you more than deserve it."

"Of course he does," said Decker.

I looked at Quint, who also stood. "Don't forget I'm the one who pushed you out of the nest and made you return to England."

"Hey, I was there too," said Decker, elbowing him.

I laughed and walked to the foyer. "Trust that I will be in touch in a couple of days, yes?" I said when they followed.

"Yes," answered Wren. "Come on, guys. Let's leave these two alone."

20

After watching them leave, I closed the door and locked it. "Now, George, let's talk about those sexy undergarments."

"Talk?" she asked.

I leaned in and kissed her for the umpteenth time, then took her hand and led her upstairs, stopping just outside the entrance to my bedroom. "Stay put. I'll just be a moment."

She smiled. "Yes, sir."

As tempted as I was to kiss her again, I let go of her hand and proceeded with my plan.

After dimming the overheads, I lit the candles I'd set out yesterday, checked the flowers like I had earlier, took a deep breath, and returned to her.

"I've dreamed of this night so many times," I said, leading her inside and over to the bed. "Tell me you want this as much as I do."

She put her hands on my chest. "I want it more, Z."

"You are so beautiful," I murmured, stroking her cheek with my fingertips. "I've never been able to resist you."

"I haven't wanted you to."

Her words sent blood pumping through my body—actually, to only one part of my body. My cock was engorged with it.

When she put her hands on the hem of her shirt to raise it, I circled her wrist with my fingers. "Let me."

Her breath hitched.

"Do you know I've spent hours imagining doing unspeakable things to you, George?"

The warm brown in her eyes was almost entirely eclipsed by the black of her dilated pupils. It was heady, this. That she wanted me as much as I wanted her.

I removed her top and tossed it on the floor. "There are countless ways I want to pleasure you."

"Z, please, I need you to touch me."

I went to my knees, and when her back arched, I nuzzled my face between her legs, then looked up at her. "Your nipples are hard. Play with them for me."

With the scent of her arousal driving me mad, I yanked everything covering the lower half of her body down her legs, then slid my fingers between her folds, exploring as much as the pants around her ankles allowed me to. I thrust two fingers into her heat, then leaned forward and circled her clit with my tongue.

George gripped my shoulders with one hand and weaved her fingers in my hair with the other.

When she did, I leaned back and stopped touching her. "I told you to play with your nipples." While my eyes were scrunched and my voice growly, I smiled.

Her legs shook when she moved her hands back to her breasts and I returned to my assault on her pussy. I licked her and lifted one leg free of its confines, then the other. She undulated under my touch as I pressed the tip of my tongue against her clit and thrust the same two fingers back inside her, crooking them.

"Let go, George. Come for me," I demanded when I felt her shattering beneath my touch. I sucked her clit harder and thrust my fingers deeper as she rode out her climax. When her head hung forward and her hands rested on my shoulders, I stood and ran my thumb over her lips so she could taste what I had.

I hissed when I felt her hand cup me and grabbed her wrist like I had earlier.

"Z, please," she whined.

"Not yet, my love."

She looked at me with hooded eyes. "Please," she said again.

"Come." I led her into the bathroom. It was far bigger than I'd ever needed, decadently luxurious, and absolutely perfect for what I had planned.

I held on to her with one hand while I started the water in the tub with the other. "As much as I like this, it's time to take it off." I ran my finger along the lace of her bra, pinched her nipple through the silk, then reached around and unfastened it.

After testing the temperature with my fingers, I guided George into the tub.

"Watch me." Her eyes trailed down my body as I shed my clothes. When I dropped my trousers and my aching cock jutted in front of me, George's breath hitched again. It was quickly becoming the sexiest thing I'd ever heard. Her eyes, still black, still imploring me, still desiring me, turned me on so fucking much I couldn't stand not touching her.

I entered the water and sat behind her when she slid forward. Once seated, I pulled her back to me and lifted her with my legs so my cock nestled between the cheeks of her arse. I reached around and covered her breasts with my palms, letting her relax against me.

My soft caresses quickly turned into tugs of desire. I pinched, then rolled the nipples between my fingertips before pinching again. George's head fell forward, and her bottom pushed against me. I shifted her body so I had access to her mouth, kissed her lips, then dragged my teeth down the side of her neck. My hands returned to her breasts, but this time, I kept my touch light. "I could do this for hours," I whispered, then tongued her ear and nibbled on its lobe. I was rewarded with her dusty rose nubs tightening and her grinding her pussy against my cock.

"Not yet, my darling," I said, moving my hands away.

The long, drawn-out sound that emanated from George's lips was somewhere between a whine and a groan when I moved her forward until our bodies no longer touched. "Lie back. I've got you." I cupped the back of her head and gently eased it lower, closer to the water, then used my other hand to dampen it.

I reached over and picked up the shampoo from the outer edges of the tile that surrounded the tub, where

I'd placed it, and drizzled it in her hair. I set it down and used both hands to massage her scalp.

"God, that feels good," she murmured.

I wanted to make her repeat those words again and again as I explored every inch of her body, massaging the bath gel into her neck, shoulders, down her arms, and over her flat stomach. I peered down at her tight nipples and decided to leave those alone for now.

After drizzling more gel onto my hands, I reached down and spread her legs. She cried out when my fingers, slick from the soap, parted her folds as I relaunched my exploration of her pussy. As crazy as I knew I was driving her, I was making myself dizzy with my pent-up need to be inside her. I stood, pulling her up with me, then let her sit on the edge of the tub.

"Do not move, George."

Her eyes were glazed when she whispered, "Yes, sir."

Instead of getting out of the tub to start the shower as I'd planned, I pulled her back to her feet and cupped her chin. "Say it again."

"Yes, sir."

I'd heard those two words spoken from her lips countless times, all in answer to an order I'd given her in my role as her boss. Never once had they excited me the way they did now.

"George…"

"Yes, sir," she repeated for the third time.

My mouth crashed into hers as desire coursed through me unlike any I'd ever known. "Do you know what those words, spoken from your lips, do to me?"

She grabbed my hand and put it between her legs. "Do you feel what they do to me?"

Her pussy was drenched, not from the water in the tub, but from her essence.

"I cannot wait any longer," I repeated, stepping over the tub's edge. I helped her do the same, then led her into the bedroom. "Are you cold?" I asked, noticing the chill bumps that appeared on her flesh.

"No, sir."

I nearly roared with want as I pushed her against the mattress. "I need you on your back, my darling, spread out for me."

She sat down, but rather than do as I'd commanded, she reached out and stroked my cock. Her touch was soft, too soft, but when she wrapped her fingers around me, tightened her grip, then leaned forward and touched the tip with her tongue, I knew I wouldn't last another second unless I stopped her. When I tried, she shook her head, slid from the bed onto her knees, then sucked me between her lips.

I gripped the sides of her head, controlling the pace as I drove in and out of her mouth.

"George, stop, I'm going to—" When she sucked even harder, my cock erupted.

21

George

"You were a very bad girl," Z said, pulling me to my feet before grabbing the back of my neck and crashing his mouth into mine. His kiss was like that of a man starved as he devoured my mouth. In all the times I'd imagined kissing Z, it was nothing like this. I expected him to be soft, gentle, and tentative. I was thrilled beyond measure that he wasn't.

He was literally the sexiest man I'd ever been with. Sexier than even my basest fantasies. I'd never dreamed he'd be so forceful, so commanding, and that he was, made me want to submit to his every desire.

When my pussy clenched and I squeezed my thighs together to ease the ache between my legs, he broke our kiss and his eyes bored into mine. "You unmanned me."

"I'm sorry, sir."

His eyes softened. "I doubt you are in the slightest."

I couldn't help but smile even as I lowered my gaze to the floor. "Honestly, I'm not."

The noise he made was low, almost growly, and when I tried to squeeze my thighs together a second time, he thrust his hand between them. "Your orgasms will come from me and only me. Do you understand?"

"Yes."

He raised a brow.

"Yes, sir."

He cupped my pussy with the palm of one hand while he held my breast with the other. "You are mine." He put two fingers inside me. "This is mine." He leaned forward and swirled one nipple, then the other, with his tongue. "These are mine." He reached around and lightly smacked my bottom. "And this is mine."

"All of me is yours, Z."

His expression, which had become increasingly possessive, changed. His eyes were warm as he leaned forward, first kissing my eyelids, then the tip of my nose, then my lips. He rested his forehead against mine. "I love you."

"I love you."

He stepped back and took my hand, leading me to the side of the bed. "We are going to make love now, George. It'll be slow but intense. Impassioned but sensual. So pleasurable, it'll be painful. Can you guess how I know this so certainly? Because I have spent hours planning, fantasizing, imagining how it would be when our bodies finally joined together." His kiss was quick and chaste. "Now, lie down for me. I want you in the middle of the bed, legs as far open as you can spread them." When I did as he said, I heard him murmur, "Good girl."

What I didn't expect was for him to walk to the end of the bed instead of joining me on it.

"I want to look at what's mine," he said as he took his cock in his hand and slowly stroked it.

My body moved on its own, my eyes begging him to touch me. Anywhere would be better than this slow, agonizing need he was intentionally building inside me.

"What do you want, my darling?"

I reached out to him. "You. Please, Z. I've waited so long." I trailed my eyes down his body, taking in his powerful arms and hands. His abs were laddered, more defined than I'd ever seen, even in photos of men half his age. His stomach was flat, and where his obliques met the transversus abdominis muscles, a perfect V-shape forced my line of sight to his rigid cock.

I nearly cried in relief when he climbed on the bed and positioned himself between my legs. My brief and temporary joy ended far too quickly when he eased away and stood. I watched him stalk to the nightstand, open the drawer, and pull out a condom. My eyes never left his, even with how much I wanted to watch him roll it on.

"Are you ready for me, George?"

"I am."

He got back on the bed and knelt between my thighs once more. "Show me."

I moved my hand down my body and spread myself with my fingers. Once wet, I held them out to him. Z grabbed my hand and brought it to his mouth.

"I will never get enough of you," he said, releasing my fingers before he stroked his cock through my wetness.

I almost came off the bed when he first pressed the tip against my engorged bundle of nerves, then entered me. The lightest touch of his finger where his cock had just been, obliterated me.

A thousand stars exploded in my mind as waves of pleasure coursed through me. I held onto his forearms when I felt my body spinning higher and higher while Z's cock and fingers led me straight to another crescendo, then another after that. I felt him still for just a moment, then thrust twice more. The look on his face, that of a man experiencing the ultimate ecstasy, brought me straight back to the brink. My pussy clenched his cock, never wanting to let go.

"My God," he muttered, all too soon shifting our bodies so he lay beside me. The emptiness I felt was soul crushing, and my eyes filled with tears.

"George? Talk to me," he whispered.

"That was, I don't even know how to describe it. Life-altering."

He smiled and cupped my cheek. "Exactly how I felt the first time we met."

"Me too," I whispered.

I drifted to sleep with Z's arms around me and my fingers woven in the hair on his chest. When I woke, I was alone. It was only after looking around, making sure I hadn't woken in my own bed after the most erotic dream I'd ever had, that I allowed myself to breathe and savor the moment, wrapped in blankets that smelled of him.

When I heard water running in the shower, I hurried into the bathroom, not wanting to miss the chance to join him. I stood, watching his gloriously naked body.

He leaned slightly forward with one hand on the tile wall, bracing himself. His eyes were closed, and it appeared he hadn't heard me, so I lingered, looking down the length of him. His legs were as defined and powerful looking as the rest of him. One was bent, hiding his penis from my gaze. Then, as if he suddenly felt my presence, he turned and looked at me.

"Can I come in?" I asked.

"I was hoping you would." He stood straight, and I could see he was as hard as he'd been earlier. I stared at the man I'd loved for so long, the one with whom I'd experienced fabulous, life-changing sex, and wondered again if I were dreaming.

His eyes sparkled, and he held his hand out to me. "Be careful what you wish for, George. I may keep you here with me, naked for all eternity."

"You'll get no argument from me," I said, rubbing up against him when he pulled me close.

"Truly?" Coupled with the look on his face, his question surprised me.

"Yes. Truly."

He wrapped his arms around my waist, and I put mine around his neck.

"I spent last night and this morning lamenting all the time I wasted not being with you. I won't waste more, George. When I said I never want you out of my sight, I meant it."

"Okay."

"Which poses a significant problem."

I cocked my head. "What?"

"I resigned my position with MI6 yesterday. I somehow doubt my replacement, even if it is Pinch, will tolerate me coming to the office with you every day, trailing behind you like the hopelessly in-love puppy dog I am."

I chuckled. "No? After witnessing his anguish when you were missing, I think Pinch will grant your every wish."

His eyes scrunched. "What about you, George? Will you grant my every wish?"

My eyes bored into his. "I will, Z."

"You may not once you hear what I'm asking."

I rested my hands on his forearms, loving the feel of the warm water against my back. "If you're asking me to leave MI5, you're too late."

He studied me but didn't speak.

"I've already decided to resign."

"You're certain of this?"

"I heeded what you said, Z, about us never being apart. Since you returning to MI6 is *entirely* out of the question, tendering my resignation is our only option."

"Entirely?"

"If you did return, I'd quit anyway."

"While this conversation is rhetorical, I'm curious why you say you'd quit."

"Because I won't go back to you being my boss. To you denying what is between us for the sake of propriety."

He brushed away the tear that rolled down my cheek. "I could never give you up. Not for anything in the world, but most especially not for propriety."

"So, what's next for us?" I asked.

"Besides more lovemaking?" He winked.

"That's a given."

"How about a strong cup of tea and a decent meal?"

With his words, my stomach grumbled. "Sorry. I haven't eaten since yesterday morning."

His eyes opened wide.

"I couldn't, Z. The idea that I'd never—"

He covered my mouth with a gentle kiss. "Shh. I'm here, and so are you. No more what-ifs, no more wasted time, no more being anywhere but together."

"Hmm."

"What?" he asked, brushing my nipple with his fingertip. "I'm not opposed to tying you to the bed to keep you with me if necessary."

I raised a brow. "Neither am I."

He smiled. "What was the hmm about?"

"I might have to return to my flat from time to time."

He turned off the shower, opened the door, and grabbed a towel that he then wrapped around me. We stepped out, and he wrapped another around himself.

"About that."

"Returning to my flat?"

"What I'm about to say may seem, um, premature."

I pulled the warm terry cloth around me tighter. "Go on."

"I want you to move in with me, George."

I took a breath to speak, but didn't when he put his fingertip on my lips.

"There's more." He put his arms around me and held me close. "Marry me, George. Be my wife. Spend your life with me."

My eyes darted back and forth between his.

"I'm serious."

"You are?" I whispered.

He nodded.

"Then, yes."

He looked up at the ceiling, then back at me. His eyes, like mine, were full of tears.

"Thank you for loving me enough to wait for me," he murmured.

"Thank you for not making me wait any longer. I would've forever, you know. That's how much I love you."

22

Z

The next day, George and I spent the morning in bed, then made a late brunch together, followed by more lovemaking. Before dark, I convinced her to go to her flat to grab whatever she'd need for the next couple of days.

While I'd anticipated George would find my proposal far too hasty, the ease with which she and I navigated around each other felt as though we'd been a couple for years rather than hours.

She also didn't appear to take exception to the fact I couldn't keep my hands off her. As she placed her clothes in a bag, I walked up behind her, moved her hair from her neck, and kissed the soft skin of her nape. Each time I put my arms around her, she'd drop whatever she was doing and eagerly fall into my embrace.

On the way back to my townhouse, I swung by the Indian restaurant where I'd intended to take her on our first date and picked up a dinner order I'd placed earlier.

"You won't miss your flat?" I asked George after we'd eaten and were sitting on the sofa in front of a roaring fire, wrapped in each other's arms.

She shrugged a shoulder. "It's a nice place."

"But?"

"You aren't the only one who thought about wasted time, Z."

"Your flat is not the only thing we need to talk about."

She tightened her arm around my waist. "I told myself nothing else mattered. I'd trade anything to have the chance at a life with you, Z. My flat, my job, anything."

While we both needed time to allow being together to sink in, there were many other things we'd need to discuss before we actually married. Primary among the topics was that of children. It wasn't something I'd bring up now, but I'd given it some thought.

Katherine and I were barely out of college when we started our family, and then she was gone. Quint and Wren were so young when she passed that I wondered if either remembered much about their mother, outside of the stories Te-Te and I had told them.

Yes, I was fifty-two, but I didn't feel too old to have more children. Whenever I thought about George carrying my child, my heart felt fuller, happier. I wanted to experience as much as I could with her—lazy days spent talking and making love, traveling the world, doing everything I'd been too busy to as chief of MI6.

George rested her hand on my chest. "You're thinking *very* hard, Z."

I smiled and kissed her forehead. "Is it that obvious?"

"It is. Anything you want to share?"

"Just thinking about life and how easy it is to get caught up in the day-to-day stuff that really doesn't matter. Then something happens that makes you realize one day has turned into ten, ten into one hundred, and before you know it, years have passed."

"I'm feeling that too, but, Z, since we can't go back and change it, why don't we make as many moments in the future matter?"

"I couldn't agree more."

George covered her mouth when she yawned.

"Time for bed, or should I say sleep?"

She smiled. "I'm sorry to say I'll likely fall asleep as soon as my head rests on the pillow."

I squeezed her, then stood and held my hand out to help her up. "I love that you're here with me."

She smiled. "Good thing since now that I am, you are never getting rid of me."

I expected I'd fall asleep as quickly as George had, but instead, I lay awake, thinking about Puck.

I didn't doubt my decision to stop Pinch from having him arrested. I finally understood that his desperation had driven him to act in the way he had. He was right when he said I would've dismissed his claims, and it shamed me. If George disappeared tomorrow, I would use every resource at my disposal and make every deal I had to in order to find her as quickly as she'd found me. Puck had never had that option, and he knew it. The chain of events, starting with Beak's and Vulcan's deaths, worked against both him and Seshat.

I vowed nothing would work against them again. I'd do everything within my power to get him the help he needed to find the woman he loved.

George shifted in her sleep so her back was to me. Rather than stare at the ceiling, I turned so her back was to my front and draped an arm around her. "I love you," I whispered.

"I love you too," she whispered back.

It was daylight when I woke the next morning. It was unusual for me to sleep this late. However, my life was entirely different than it had been forty-eight hours ago. The most important and significant change was the woman sleeping in bed beside me. The one who I'd woken twice more to make love to last night.

"You're awake," George said, rolling to her back and stretching her arms over her head.

"I am." I leaned forward and kissed her. "How did you sleep?"

"Quite well, thanks. Even though someone kept waking me up." She shifted and winced.

"What's wrong?"

"Nothing. I'm a bit sore is all."

I grimaced. "Apologies."

"Don't you dare say you're sorry. As you are abundantly aware, I enjoyed every minute of making love with you."

I beamed. "Likewise."

After showering together, we went downstairs to make breakfast. While I started the kettle, George got two cups out and set them on the counter.

"I hope you don't mind me making myself at home."

I crowded her against the counter and leaned in for a kiss. "Mind? It's my strongest desire. Wait, not my *strongest*, but up there."

The kettle began to whistle, so I released her, removed it from the heat, and took the cream I knew she liked from the refrigerator.

She stirred her tea and studied me. "What's on your mind, Z?"

"Yesterday, you mentioned leaving MI5. In fact, Pinch said you already had."

"We talked about it, yes. I haven't submitted my resignation yet, although I intend to."

"I want you to know that a relationship between us is not predicated on you resigning if you don't want to. I mean, I know you're of your own mind, of course."

"I've given it a lot of thought, and I don't want to stay at MI5."

"Understood."

She smirked. "Do not be so quick to say you do."

I chuckled. "No?"

George shook her head. "While I no longer want to work at Vauxhall Cross. I had another idea."

"Go on."

"What would you think about approaching Wren and Wilder about joining up with them?"

"An interesting thought." Actually, it was brilliant. By going private, there would be limited red tape and, for me, far less administrative work. Also, we could pick and choose what we wanted to take on.

"They're currently devoting a great deal of time to the AMPS investigation, but I feel certain Nemesis would approve the additional expenditure to bring us on in a different capacity. And, Z…"

I'd been lost in thought but looked up at her. "Yes?"

"While I will respect your decision if you say you want to leave intelligence entirely, I know you well enough to believe you truly don't."

"You're absolutely right. It's the bureaucracy I've no interest in."

"What about workplace romance?"

I put my hand on the back of her neck and kissed her. "I'm highly in favor of it."

She took a sip of tea. "There's something else I want to talk to you about."

"What's on your mind, George?" I asked, grinning that I'd repeated her words back to her.

"You mentioned me missing my flat."

"Right. Well, if you don't want to give it up, we could—"

George covered my mouth with her hand. "I wasn't finished."

I kissed her palm before she let go. "Apologies."

"While my flat isn't all that important to me, there's another place that is. When my parents passed away, I inherited the home I grew up in. It's a bit of a drive from London, so I don't visit it as often as I'd like."

"Where is it?"

"Not far from Whittaker Abbey."

"Is that right? Very conveniently located should we partner up with Wilder and Wren."

"I understand if you don't want to leave London—"

"What was it you said a few minutes ago about not being too quick to say you understand something before you actually do?"

She cocked her head and smirked. "Yes?"

"I'm not opposed to leaving London. Not at all, actually."

"Would you like to take a look at it?"

"Love to. When?"

"I don't know. Whenever it's convenient."

I looked at my watch. "Would an hour from now be considered convenient?"

George beamed. "You really want to go now?"

"I can't think of anything I'd rather do. Well, except take you back to bed, of course."

"Rest assured there are beds at Woburn House. Several, in fact."

My eyes opened wide. "Woburn House?"

George put her hand on mine. "Yes, although not to be confused with Woburn Castle."

"I'm familiar with both."

"If you'd rather not—"

I stood and pulled her up with me. "I'd rather."

Once again, George beamed, melting my heart.

23

George

I'd spent years wanting to be with Z, and now that we were together—as brief as it was thus far—it seemed…easy. The sex alone was mind-blowing. It was more than that, though. We just got on.

I was reminded of something my mum had said to me years ago. I was a teenager at the time, fresh out of a breakup and quite melancholy about it.

She sat me down and told me a story about when she met my father. She said she realized quite quickly that every other relationship she'd been in was a struggle. I clearly remembered her saying that from their first date, things between her and my father were the opposite. She no longer felt the push and pull she'd experienced previously. "This is the part I want you to heed, Leighton. Relationships are work, yes, but they shouldn't feel like a constant battle of wits."

I recalled thinking my mum was quite naive or perhaps not looking at her relationship with my father realistically. Thinking back on it, though, I'd never seen the two in a heated argument. What I'd witnessed were discussions. Some had ended in agreeing to disagree, but they were always respectful.

Perhaps for Z and me, it was more the maturity that came with age. Maybe it was that we'd spent so much time pining for each other that we appreciated every moment.

When Z asked me to marry him, he'd prefaced it by saying I may find what he was about to say premature. I hadn't. Not in the slightest. When he'd asked, I didn't hesitate to tell him I'd marry him. Even now, it felt so natural, so perfect—so right.

Time would tell, of course, but whenever I looked into his eyes, I saw love.

"You're deep in thought," he said, reaching over to cover my hand with his on our drive to Woburn House.

"Thinking about how happy I am."

He grinned, brought my hand to his lips, and kissed my palm. "As am I. Brilliantly so." He cleared his throat. "There is one thing I want to discuss with you. It's about Christmas."

I turned to face him. "Go on."

"I'd planned to spend it at the ranch in Texas. Quint and Decker both live there with their families. Actually,

Decker's ranch is adjacent, but I digress. It's something we talked about several weeks ago. Wren and Wilder intend to bring Katherine. It will be the first time we're all together as a family in several years."

"It sounds lovely."

"Yeah? And perhaps you and I could share a romantic getaway after? Just the two of us?"

"Equally lovely."

"You're sure?" he asked.

"Absolutely. Are you not?"

Z turned on a side road, drove a short way, then parked the car.

"Where are we?" I asked.

"Nowhere, it's just…" He took both my hands in his. "Katherine and I married on New Year's Eve, and while it seems fitting that you and I start out the next year as husband and wife—"

"What about on Christmas?" I blurted. Not that I'd given the idea any thought. It just came to me, and when it did, it seemed perfect. "Unless I'm rushing things."

"Rushing things? I'd marry you tomorrow if the blasted UK didn't impose a waiting period."

"Right. That would make a Christmas wedding somewhat difficult."

He smiled broadly. "Not in Texas."

Woburn House never failed to take my breath away. It was so grand it was daunting. However, each generation, my parents' included, had updated both the interior and the grounds, so it had a far warmer feel than many other estates in Bedfordshire.

The exterior architecture was quite ornate, which was reflected in the interior walls by way of archways, nooks, and crannies, but my mum's decorating style was casual and cozy.

The kitchens—there were two—had both been updated, as had the bathrooms. The formal dining room, with walls hung in a deep-red damask paper, was quite gaudy, in my opinion. If I lived on the estate full-time, it would be the first room I'd redo.

To me, this had always been home, but seeing it through Z's eyes gave me a different perspective. Was it too much? While his townhouse was in Mayfair, one of the poshest areas in all of London, it wasn't ornate by any means. This was.

"What do you think?" I asked, unable to stand his silent reflection any longer.

"It's quite beautiful."

"But?"

For the second time on our drive, Z stopped the car. From where we were parked, we had a full view of the entrance to Woburn House and the park-like grounds that led up to it. He cut the engine. "Tell me what it was like growing up here."

"Quite normal, actually."

He raised a brow. "Normal?"

"I mean, my parents rarely hosted parties like some of the neighboring estates did. We just *lived*, if that makes any sense."

"Perfect sense. The ranch in Texas belonged to my late wife's family and is one of the largest in Texas. I would imagine if you asked Quint and Wren what it was like to grow up there, they'd probably say something similar. It's where they lived."

"Would you like to see the inside?"

"In a moment." Z seemed lost in thought.

"Is everything all right?"

He turned to me, took my hand, and kissed my palm. "More than. I was just imagining you as a girl, playing outside." He pointed to a large tree from which hung a swing. "There, for example."

I smiled. "My dad put that up for me, and you're right; I adored it."

Rather than release my hand, Z stroked the back of it with his thumb. "You were an only child."

I nodded. "Yes. I did have an older brother, but he passed before I was born."

His grip on my hand tightened. "I'm so sorry."

"It was obviously far harder on my parents, given I never knew him. He wasn't a year old when he died. He had a heart defect that made it inevitable."

"Tragic."

My parents rarely talked about him, but they often visited his grave. From a window in the back of the house, I could see them in the family cemetery. My father's arm would be around my mum's shoulders, and I knew they were both crying. "It was," I murmured.

"There's something I need to ask you, and I want you to promise you'll be honest before you answer."

"Okay…"

"How do you feel about having children, George?"

The air briefly left my lungs. His question shouldn't have taken me by surprise. Z was always forthright. I would've been honest whether he made me promise to be or not. It was something I'd thought quite a lot about in the years I dreamed of Z and I being together.

"It's something I let go of quite some time ago."

His penetrating gaze made me want to look away.

"Why?"

"Do you really have to ask?" I turned my head, focusing on the swing where I'd spent so many hours of my childhood.

He squeezed my hand. "Look at me, George."

I took a deep breath and faced him. "I want to be with *you* more than anything. When I thought…" My voice was choked with emotion. "Sorry."

"Don't be. Tell me what you're feeling."

"I tried very hard not to think the worst. However, there were times I feared I'd never see you again."

"I feared I'd never see you again, either."

"All I wanted was for you to come back to me. Not just come back. But *to me*. That's all that mattered."

"And I did. If I recall correctly, it took me all of thirty seconds to declare my undying love for you."

I smiled. "While hardly that dramatic, I must say, it was a dream come true to hear you say you love me."

"I do, you know? So much it feels my heart will burst." He leaned closer to me. If anything, his gaze intensified. "I want to experience everything with you, George. *Everything.*"

"What are you saying?"

"A family. Children. Watching as my child grows inside you, then raising him or her as well as their siblings here, at Woburn House."

"I thought…"

He chuckled. "That I was too old?"

I squeezed his hand like he had mine. "No. I just thought you wouldn't want more children."

"I do, my darling, very much, in fact."

"I do too, Z." I grinned. "On the other hand, you are a grandfather, so perhaps somewhere in the back of my mind, I did imagine you too old."

Z laughed again, then put his hand on the back of my neck and pulled me close enough to kiss. "You little minx. I may see a punishment in your near future. Pleasurable, but a punishment, nonetheless."

God in heaven, why did his words make my pussy clench?

He studied me. "I see you like that idea."

My cheeks flushed, and I lowered my gaze. Z put his fingertips on my chin. "Look at me, my darling."

I shook my head first, but did as he asked.

"What is between us will always be *making love*. Regardless of what excites us, that is at the core. There is no shame or embarrassment if we love each other."

When his fingers brushed my nipple, my breath hitched and I squeezed my thighs together.

"You did assure me there were several beds, yes?"

"Yes, sir." My voice sounded breathy, filled with desire.

"God, what it does to me when you say that."

I glanced down at his hardness straining against his trousers. When I reached out to stroke it, Z caught my wrist with one hand. "Not yet, my love. First a tour. Perhaps starting with the bedrooms?"

24

Z

George and I spent the next few weeks moving out of my townhouse and her flat, and into Woburn House. Truth be told, I felt more at home there than anywhere else I'd ever lived. Perhaps it wasn't the residence at all. It was the woman who, in less than a week's time, would be my wife. Being with her was the happiest I'd been in my entire life.

Of course I'd been happy with Katherine, thrilled when our two children were born, but life with George was different. It could be attributed to my, ahem, advanced age and the fact I was no longer concerned with making a name for myself with SIS, but something told me that regardless of our circumstances, I would be content, even at peace, as long as George was by my side.

Contentment, however, did not mean either of us were bored. We made love day and night, neither of us able to keep our hands off each other. When we weren't pleasuring each other's bodies, we talked, explored the estate, and sat in the Woburn House's library, where floor-to-ceiling shelves were full of books. I'd light the fire, and the two of us would cozy up and read. There'd been many times when we ended up stretched out on a blanket that I'd laid on the floor in front of the fireplace, both of us naked.

George thrived under my dominant nature, something I'd never indulged in before being with her. Thus, the sex was the best of my life.

"You've got that dreamy look in your eyes again," said George, wrapping her arms around my neck.

I put my arms around her waist and pulled her body flush with mine. "I'm a man in love."

She smiled when my hardness pressed against her. "As much as just being in your arms drives me wild with desire, we've a plane to catch."

"I suppose it wouldn't do to miss our flight."

George chuckled. "Your daughter would be quite put out with us. She might even insist they hold the plane."

I cupped her cheek and kissed her. "By this time next week, you and I will be married."

"If it's too soon—"

I silenced her with another kiss, then patted her stomach. "Who knows? There could be a little Leighton or Archer already percolating in there."

George shook her head, but her smile was from ear to ear. "I love you, Archer."

"I love you, Leighton."

"I don't remember us being like that," I heard my daughter say to Wilder once George and I were seated next to each other on the private aircraft that would take us from London to Austin, Texas. My arm was around her, and her hand rested on my leg. Every so often, I'd lean in and kiss her.

He looked up from the book he was reading. "We were. In fact, we are."

"I've got four years to make up for," I said, kissing George twice more.

We hadn't told Wren, Quint, or Decker about our plans to marry or that we were letting nature take its course with trying to conceive. When I followed George's line of sight over to baby Katherine, I squeezed her tight against me. Yes, I wanted children very much. But more so for my soon-to-be wife. The day I'd asked her thoughts on the subject, I saw the longing in her eyes, as much as she tried to mask it.

The sun had set by the time we reached the ranch. As we pulled up to the main entrance, I saw Quint and Decker had gone all out this year. The gate itself was adorned with lights and garland, and on either side of the road leading to the barns were massive light displays. One was of a cowboy on horseback, and another was a heifer with her calf. There were Christmas trees made solely of lights, shooting stars, an animated display of a couple of elves making toys, and flying reindeer. Right before we reached the main house, Santa and Mrs. Claus, again depicted only in sparkling lights, were on display next to the barn they towered above.

"This is brilliant," I heard George whisper. Her eyes wide, and her smile dazzling.

"We've done it every year for the families of the people who work the ranch, but it's never been this elaborate," said Wren.

"I have a feeling the older our children get, the more extravagant it will be," added Wilder.

I had one arm around George's shoulders and rested my other hand on her stomach. I couldn't explain it, but I just knew she was pregnant. It was too early on for a test to confirm it, but I attributed it to a father's intuition.

Decker, Mila, and Huck were waiting with Quint, Darrow, and Wells when Wilder pulled up in front of the house. We'd all have dinner together here tonight before going to the guesthouses where we'd stay while visiting.

Quint had offered up the main house, but I told him that it was his and Mila's home now. It hadn't been mine for a very long time. More importantly, it had never been George's and mine.

That Katherine and I had begun our life together in the townhouse was one reason I hadn't wanted to make that our main residence. George had said what happened in the past didn't bother her. However, as I told her, I wanted to make memories in places that meant something to both of us.

"Ready for this?" I asked after I'd exited the vehicle and held my hand out to George to do the same.

"If you are." We'd agreed to announce our plans to marry once all of us were together. I had no doubt everyone would be thrilled for us. Like me with them, the only thing any of us wanted was for the people we loved to be happy. I was that in spades.

Once we were seated at the table in the main dining room, which was rarely used, I stood and held up the glass of wine Quint had poured. "I have an important announcement, everyone."

I held my love's hand when she stood beside me. Wren's eyes opened wide when she noticed George's glass was filled with water. "We're getting married," I blurted, knowing if I didn't, Wren would beat me to the punch by asking if we were expecting.

As I'd anticipated, there were shouts of congratulations from everyone at the table, followed by hugs for both George and me.

"Are you making any other announcements tonight, Daddy?" Wren whispered.

"Not tonight," I said with a wink.

"So, when's the weddin'?" Decker asked after we were all seated again.

I looked at George. "Christmas Day," she responded.

"*This* Christmas?" Quint asked. "In three days?"

I nodded. "Which means we will go to Austin tomorrow to secure the license."

"They seem pleased," said George, smiling.

The two of us sat and listened to the rest of those at the table talk over one another in their excitement to make plans for our wedding day.

"Perhaps overzealous would be a better word," I whispered.

"I hope this won't eclipse Christmas," she whispered back.

"Huck and Wells won't care. They'll probably be as interested in the brightly colored wrapping paper as they are in the gifts," said Deck, who was seated on the opposite side of me and must've overheard George's concern. "A couple years from now, they'll be all about Santa comin' down the chimney." He cleared his throat and looked up at the ceiling.

"Are you all right?" I asked.

"Hell yeah. I was just thinkin' about the first Christmas I spent with y'all." He looked around me at George. "Z here got all decked out in a Santa suit, even though we were old enough to know it was him."

"I think we were thirteen," said Quint.

"I know we were because I hadn't celebrated a single Christmas until that year. Let me tell you, Z, Quint, and Wren more than made up for it."

"And Te-Te," said Wren when the woman walked into the dining room with a platter of the kind of steak you can only get in Texas.

"Mr. Decker was such a sweet boy back then," Te-Te said, pinching his cheek after he took the platter from her arms and set it on the table.

"One year, we're gonna get you to join us for dinner," I said when I stood to greet her. "Maybe on Christmas." I motioned to George, who stood and walked over to us. "Te-Te, I'd like you to meet George, the woman I'm marrying in three days."

She covered her mouth when she gasped, then hugged me. "Oh, Mr. Z, I am so happy for you." Her eyes were filled with tears when she took George's hands in hers. "Mr. Z is a wonderful man, and I know just by looking in your eyes that you are an equally wonderful woman."

I put my arm around her. "You have always taken such good care of my family as well as all those who work here and their families. Te-Te is the head cook at the dining hall."

George smiled, still holding Te-Te's hands. "We would be honored if you would join us for the wedding."

Te-Te gasped a second time, her eyes filled with tears, and she nodded. "I am the one who would be honored."

"Where is the wedding, Dad?" Quint asked.

"In the courtyard, under all the twinkling lights," Te-Te said, pointing across the room at the windows that looked out on the place she suggested before I had the chance to respond. It wasn't where I'd planned, but it was a far better idea.

I glanced at George, and her smile told me she was all for it.

Two nights later, she and I sat in front of the Christmas tree Quint and Decker had put up in this guesthouse to match the one in the house where Wilder and Wren were staying. I'd lit a fire, and we were both sipping hot cocoa.

"Katherine and I used to do this on Christmas Eve. When the kids were very little, late nights were often the only time we could talk."

George snuggled closer to me but didn't say anything.

"I hope I'm not being disrespectful by bringing it up."

She shook her head. "Not at all."

"Even if we're sitting here on Christmas Eve, staring at the tree like she and I used to do?"

"It's not the same tree, Z. And you're not the same man. Katherine may have gotten you first, but I got you for always."

"I was going to wait and give this to you tomorrow, but I'm too impatient." I removed my arm from around her shoulders, pulled the small box from my pocket, and got down on one knee. "Leighton 'George' Marietta, you appeared when I least expected it, like an angel bringing me back to life and loving me in a way I've never experienced. You're patient, kind, sexy, and beautiful. Smart, funny, and the best part is you're all mine." I opened the box and held it in front of her. "Will you marry me tomorrow?"

She looked from the ring to me, then back again. I couldn't read her expression, but if I had to, I'd say she was confused. "George, is everything all right?"

She laughed and cried simultaneously. "Everything is perfect. So perfect."

"Shall I take that as a yes?"

"Yes! Of course yes!" She wrapped her arms around my neck and kissed me. It was the kind of kiss that always led to the two of us naked, with our bodies joined together. So when she broke that kiss, stood, and told me she'd be right back, I didn't know what to think.

I looked down at the ring that still sat nestled in the box. Maybe she didn't care for it. I rested on my haunches, unsure what I should do next.

When she returned, she also had a ring box in her hand. She sat closer to the Christmas tree and held her hand out to me.

"I planned to give this to you tomorrow as well, but after seeing the ring you chose for me, I cannot wait." She took my left hand in hers, opened the box, removed the ring, and slid it on my third finger.

When I gazed down at it, every doubt left my mind. Both of us had chosen the same ring for each other. Thick platinum bands, hers with a three-carat diamond set in the center while the one in mine was far smaller. Both stones were surrounded by the same design, etched into the band. *Angel wings.*

"Marry me, Z?"

"Yes, my love. I will marry you." I slid her ring on the third finger of her left hand, then kissed her like she had me.

Minutes later, we were both naked, stretched out in front of the tree, the warmth of the fire at our backs, making love.

Keep reading for a sneak peek
at the next book in Heather Slade's
K19 Allied Intelligence Series,
Code Name: Zeppelin

A man of silence.
A man of rigid precision. Zeppelin is your
worst nightmare, coming in quiet, and
wreaking havoc on his enemies.

1

Zeppelin

"Next order of business. Verity confirmed shortly before I requested we gather together that AMPS' Mauritian accounts were closed and the money was transferred to Switzerland. She and Zeppelin will be traveling there this afternoon to determine if it is worth relocating his task force as well as any support they might need," announced Nemesis, the commander of the UN Coalition Against Human Trafficking and my superior.

Had she not made the announcement in a room crowded with my colleagues, including those who served under me on the Swiss task force, I would've asked if she was out of her bloody mind.

Verity, the bane of my existence, had recently been promoted to Unit 23—the UK's most secretive and deadly team of intelligence agents. I was happy for her when that unit's commander had made the announcement, but happier for me. Until then, she'd been a member of my team. I'd say she was a subordinate, but that was a role she'd refused to take. In fact, more often than not, she behaved as if she was the commander rather than me.

Every word she uttered made me crazy. It was almost as if she argued with me just for the sake of doing so. The number of times I'd wanted to throttle her was only equal to one other thing—how often I'd wanted to strip her bare and fuck her senseless.

"I want to speak with the two of you," Nemesis said when Verity and I came at her from opposite directions.

Thank God. Nem had seen the error of her ways, and instead of Verity and I working together, the woman would be reassigned.

"Zeppelin, while I would normally leave it to you to craft your mission, in this case, I'm going to make a suggestion."

My eyes widened. In the world of intelligence, when a commander uttered the word "suggestion," it was widely accepted to mean "demand."

"We've received intelligence indicating there may be a lead to follow in Saint Moritz."

"Saint Moritz?" Both Verity and I gasped at the same time.

"You and Verity will be going undercover as a couple on their honeymoon."

She had to be joking. By the look on Verity's face, she agreed.

"Ma'am, you cannot be serious," Verity ventured.

"I could not be more so." Nemesis walked away. Was it my imagination, or was the woman smirking?

About the Author

USA Today and Amazon Top 15 Bestselling Author Heather Slade writes shamelessly sexy, edge-of-your seat romantic suspense.

She gave herself the gift of writing a book for her own birthday one year. Fifty-plus books later (and counting), she's having the time of her life.

The women Slade writes are self-confident, strong, with wills of their own, and hearts as big as the Colorado sky. The men are sublimely sexy, seductive alphas who rise to the challenge of capturing the sweet soul of a woman whose heart they'll hold in the palm of their hand forever. Add in a couple of neck-snapping twists and turns, a page-turning mystery, and a swoon-worthy HEA, and you'll be holding one of her books in your hands.

She loves to hear from my readers. You can contact her at heather@heatherslade.com

To keep up with her latest news and releases, please visit her website at www.heatherslade.com to sign up for her newsletter.